HELIOS

HELIOS

GRAEME BENNETT

Published by Graeme Bennett Ltd.

CONTENTS

About this book

Forward

1 The Sunflower Belt 9

2 Sunrise 20

3 Corona 31

4 Recovery 39

5 Prominence 46

6 Pink and Blue 54

7 Change of Plans 60

8 Clampdown 66

9 Looking Glass 74

CONTENTS

10 | Frigg 82

11 | Reconnaissance 92

12 | Seahaven 97

13 | Solar Storm 109

14 | 2435: Homecoming 122

15 | Retrospective 140

16 | Ad Astra 148

17 | The Well-Dressed Man 157

18 | The Tangler 171

19 | Reconstruction 180

20 | Restoration 196

21 | Wake Up Call 202

22 | A Perfect Day 214

23 | The Infinity Machine 221

24 | Perihelion 229

25 | The Valley of Decision 235

26 | The Secret Mission 244

27 | Hero City 255

28 | The Green Dome 262

29 | The Thirteenth Day 273

Afterward

RECOMMENDED READING 285

About this book

A secret experiment in 1947 leads to contact with scientists and military strategists from the 25th century and a string of events that leads our story to a variety of colorful locations around the world and beyond. You'll visit ASTRA headquarters in Houston, Texas, the offshore nation-state of Seahaven and a mysterious area about 26 miles southeast of Corona, New Mexico. You'll see the Temple of the Sun in Beijing, a robotic production line in MegaFactory City, a secret facility on the Volga river in Russia, the birthplace of Muhammed in the Middle East and the far side of the moon, too.

Enjoy the scenery!
Graeme Bennett
November 16, 2023

Forward

In the 20th century, researchers for the first time successfully measured scientifically meaningful time dilation effects and proved Einstein's time dilation predictions in his special theory of relativity. Some of these effects, such as those produced with argon-gas tubes and excimer lasers, were little more than scientific curiosities. However, by the middle of the 21st century, scientists working independently on quantum field projects in Germany and the U.S. both managed to produce effects that evidentially supported the mathematical postulation that it is possible to displace an object from its default space-time coordinates. This is the story of what happens next.

When the HELX high energy large accelerator project team began using AI-based code generators, a combination of clever code, radical reinterpretation of Einstein's space-time equations and extraordinarily good luck had produced the most extraordinary effect: a multidimensional wavefield algorithm that created time displacement effects, albeit in the forward direction only.

Under the direction of project lead Erich Rössler, a team of scientists and engineers developed and refined a top-secret system capable of "fast-forwarding" time within a highly specific region, known as a 'time bubble'.

The discovery of this temporal displacement effect naturally led to other key discoveries, the most important of which was the ability to send one-half of an entangled qubit pair forward, and maintain communications with its companion qubit that remained in the past.

This technology had proven extremely difficult to implement. It seemed, for a long time, that the so-called "no-communications theorem' was blocking all potential solutions. However, with help from the nascent Aeronautics and Space-Time Research Administration (ASTRA) division of NASA, the engineers finally solved the problem by using a method known as quantum teleportation, but with a distance factor of zero. Using this method, they were able to develop 'Qmunications'—a quantum communications module with a capability to encode text, graphics and other data types and send this information over the temporal backchannel back to the present from the future.

The members of the HELX team then reconvened to work on the final phase of the project: the ability to redirect the temporal displacement effects through the backchannel to any arbitrary location.

Needless to say, the coordinate calculations were not trivial, even with the help of an advanced AI system known as XAVR. The main challenge was to synchronize the temporal and spatial data with an exact location. When you factor in all the variables, the complexity becomes apparent: Earth is spinning at roughly 1,000 miles per hour (at the equator), traveling on its orbit around the sun at approximately 67,062 miles per hour, in a galaxy that is itself moving at an estimated 828,000 km/hr. Complicating these measurements were other factors, such as minor inconsistencies in the earth's planetary axis. For these reasons, the safest places to attempt temporal relocations were in the sky or in the ocean. And while oceans were frequently turbulent, they were generally far more predictable than the notoriously volatile atmosphere.

So, when XAVR had finally finished its calculations, they decided that the first round of temporal displacement tests would take place in the Atlantic Ocean.

Test series #2, it was hoped, would be a set of atmospheric tests, with series #3 slated for deployment in space, in near-earth orbit.

If a sufficient number of these tests were successful, it was hoped that series #4 might aim for a ground-to-ground deployment. And beyond that, human tests....

After much testing, they eventually produced a 'Transit pod' capable of sending humans and other cargo forward in time, where the module sent forward could transmit status information to a 'receiver' module still in the present. (This was before full awareness of the relative meaninglessness of terms like 'backward' and 'forward' was fully understood.)

With the realization that Einstein's statement about time being dimensional "like space" actually meant that time itself was not one-dimensional, work on a fully-realized mathematical model of multidimensional time led to the next big breakthrough: a ranged reception platform that allowed upcoming ('forward') temporal data to be targeted in the multidimensional space-time continuum and redirected to any arbitrary location within a limited range by any active portal. This was achieved by exploiting electromagnetic induction to produce high energy static fields extending from the Earth's magnetic core out through the ionosphere, essentially using the rotating Earth as a homopolar generator, then directing the resultant field effect(s) to the desired spatial coordinates. By modulating multiple wavefields, the necessary UHF fields necessary for temporal displacement were produced without requiring a dedicated base station. In essence, the magnetosphere itself became the base station. This tech directly enabled mobile devices such as the 'anywhere/anytime' Bubblecraft and the ASTRA-funded Starjumper.

Initially, it had been hoped that these technologies would lead to commercial products. But the main funding source was Cornerstone, a military-affiliated division of the U.S. government that insisted on secrecy. And so, their efforts remained top secret.

* * *

After the early experiments in quantum field generation proved the technology worthy of further research, it was discovered that government scientists had intentionally disturbed the fabric of space-time for the first time in 1947. Concerns emerged about the implications of fracturing multiple parallel quantum realities, leading risk advisors to advocate a general policy of avoidance of all contact with other-dimensional entities. Interactions with any component of another quantum reality, it was feared, could lead to permanent changes in our plane of reality, due to the effect now known as Multiplanar Field Fragmentation.

This restrictive policy began to change in the first half

of the 23rd century, when new government incentives for neurally augmented scientists led to attempts to deliberately manipulate reality in attempts to store nuclear radiation in another dimension by sending it a parallel reality, where it no longer affected our earth. Early successes in this area led to further research and, by mid-century, these experiments led to the first working implementation of localized timeshifting, in which the nuclear decay period was artificially accelerated.

For almost sixty years, only time-forward shifts had been thought possible. Finally, with the development of MDM "multi-D marker" technology, multi-dimensional shifts in time were proven to be possible in both directions.

Early tests of this tech were cut short when the government, fearful of potentially disastrous consequences from space-time paradox problems, banned all further research in this area in the 2220s.

This period was also a time of great change in the human species, as hybridized intelligence augmentation technologies led to rapid advances in genetic manipulation techniques, leading to a nearly continuous state of artificially accelerated evolution that lasted until the period of disruption caused by the unprecedented solar storms of 2431–42.

* * *

The devastating environmental changes and genetic aftermath of the unusual solar cycle of the 11-year period lasting from 2431 through 2442 led to significant corruptions of the already-diminished genomic pool that led to a crisis requiring major changes to the standard human genome.

This was the period in which hybridized humans began

to emerge in a range of post-human meta-species. A range of adaptations became common, often correlating with the environmental conditions of specific locales or climate conditions. As climate changes across the globe had accelerated during the 22nd and 23rd centuries, these groups had come to dominate, and in some cases, displace the original inhabitants in these hostile climates.

And, of course, this wasn't natural selection at work. This was technological one-upmanship, as competing nation-states and corporate entities pursued their own unique ideological endgames, resulting in the emergence of several new post-human subspecies, including the so-called Blues, the Neo-gens, and the Aquatics.

* * *

1

The Sunflower Belt

There are no particles, there are only fields
—Art Hobson

Monday, December 21, 2434
2:12 p.m.

It had been a long detour. Karl Schraeder, Li Yan Zhang, Susan Everett and the others on the team of engineers and programmers working on the High Energy Large Accelerator project known as HELX had been chasing possible answers to a question that had long eluded researchers: could they somehow use the quantum teleportation-based communication system codeveloped by their brilliant colleague George Gunderson and the division of NASA known as ASTRA

(Aeronautics and Space-Time Research Administration), to work with matter as well as information?

It seemed as though it should be possible. Their original breakthrough, way back in 2030, was to discover how to send matter (and, eventually, themselves) forward in time. Then, they learned how to send one half of an entangled pair of qubits forward in time, where users in the future could use the quantum mechanics phenomenon Einstein called "spooky action at a distance" to interact with it. The entangled particles sent forward could then be manipulated to send signals back to the particles still in the present. It wasn't exactly like sending data into the past, but it was the next best thing. This "Qmunications" technology had tremendous strategic and military potential, of course. But it only seemed to work with information—not matter.

Now, more than 400 years later, they still struggled with the challenge of somehow combining both of these effects to achieve the goal of sending matter back in time.

The proposed solution had gotten more complicated, as these things do, as the requirements were defined. Not only was encoding all the atoms of a test object as entangled bit-pairs a massively complex operation (complicated by the fact that the uncertainty principle meant that indirect measurement was required for each and every qubit), but the method was impractical for all but the simplest test cases.

It was only when the HELX team discarded that idea and switched to what they would later refer to as the "multi-D marker" (MDM) method that significant progress was made.

MDM promised to be an elegant solution to a key problem

with time-jumping: If you move an object a second or two forward in time, you have to consider that the earth itself it rotating, the planet is orbiting the sun, the solar system is moving in a spiraling galaxy, and on and on. Too many moving parts.

The MDM solution was to set a positional space-time 'sync' marker that traveled with the location itself. That way, the alignment was (mostly) assured and the number of variables greatly reduced. And so, work on developing a geo-magnetic marker became the focus.

The next challenge was how to produce the high-frequency wavefield without requiring a dedicated base station. This was accomplished by producing the sync marker via an electromagnetic induction effect in the Earth's magnetosphere. They were then able to amplify and modulate the HELX accelerator's quantum field effects and combine this technology with the backchannel transmission tech that the team had developed to generate the required field effect in the past. Because it was only the math required to calculate the necessary vector equations and field values that was being transmitted across the temporal backchannel, it managed to avoid the limitations of the "no-communications" theorem, while still delivering acceptable levels of performance. In essence, they were moving a time-position marker instead of having to send all the bits for the thing itself over the backchannel. It seemed like pure quantum-mechanical weirdness to discover that past, present, and an ever-branching set of future realities could all exist simultaneously. But there they were: many worlds.

One of the things the team had discovered during the initial round of HELX experiments was that there were certain target frequencies that 'resonated' in the time-space continuum. By isolating and amplifying these specific frequencies and using them as carrier waves for other wavefield information, they found that a relatively straightforward Boolean math operation yielded a phase-cancellation effect in the wavefield, where neither the source nor the carrier waves appeared in the output. Instead, the output was the UHF energy field producing the temporal displacement effect.

Susan Everett, the mathematician primarily responsible for this particular breakthrough, remembered the post-mortem code review that she and the others on the team had with their first boss, Erich Rössler, the day after the time displacement effect was first noted.

"But how does this resonance lead to the experimental results we've seen?" he had asked her.

"You should probably talk to George about the field dynamics themselves," she had replied. After all, George was the programmer and engineer primarily responsible for much of the code that made the quantum field generator so efficient for its size.

"But," she continued, "it was George's explanation that first got me thinking outside the box like that. He said: 'we're decoupling the notion of speed equals distance. In our equation, speed equals frequency, and our frequency is gated by the field stability.' So, I started looking into how he was doing that and, as you probably know, it's those resonance values we came up with that create the effect.

"I came up with a generalized algorithm to create stable

fields and, as it turned out, the values found to be most stable were those programmed with a very specific fractal algorithm that happened to exactly map to the Fibonacci sequence. But the interesting thing there is: those resonant values are all on a curve—they're all irrational fractal values. It's not a binary math equation at all. It's more like modeling this infinitely complex five-dimensional analog field with vectors instead of absolute numbers. Plus, we have George's brilliant routine that counteracts the Cherenkov[1] effect that had been a limiting factor.

"So, we end up with what we call the sunflower spiral belt that we build with the field equation, and the intersecting Fibonacci spirals of the sunflower belt are what produces the effect. And of course, I was as surprised as anyone as to what that effect would be when we jumped forward that first time. More surprised, probably."

[1] Sometimes spelled **Čerenkov**

Now, all these years after that initial breakthrough, they were finally ready to begin testing.

The project executives at the "consortium of consortiums" known as Cornerstone were in attendance, as they had been with increasing regularity as the target date loomed closer. The execs, all of which happened to be high-ranking U.S. military personnel, were adamant that test #1 had to take place in the air—presumably to justify some Air Force-related budget requirement. Because the Air Force had a base relatively close to the Novelty Hill jump-point and test lab where many of the team were working, it was decided that the initial round of atmospheric tests would take place in the area near the base, about 9.1 miles south-southwest of Tacoma, Washington.

Karl Schraeder, the team's lead developer, had come up with a clever routine that allowed values to be offset from the sync marker itself. This meant that the tests didn't have to take place directly at the location of the marker—using the magnetosphere and ionosphere to modulate the quantum radar signal allowed considerable latitude (literally) in where the field produced its temporal displacement effect.

He had also been working on an idea that engineering team leader Li Yan had suggested: Why not automatically string together jump values of different lengths to allow jumps to any arbitrary date, instead of only those that mapped to a single Fibonacci resonance value? Great idea, everyone had agreed. Unfortunately, testing hadn't even begun on this and time had run out. They had to get this first series of proof-of-concept tests for the brass at Cornerstone out of the way first. Then, maybe, he would have time to get it working properly.

Monitoring equipment was installed on the highest peak in the area, on the Columbia Crest summit of Mount Rainier, about forty miles to the southeast. Karl, Li Yan, and several members of the team, including a young equipment technician by the name of Frigg and a lab assistant named Leonid, assembled at Sunrise, about seven miles northeast of the mountain for the final preparations.

People were always asking Frigg whether she was related to Karl. She had to explain that, no, the reason they both had blue skin was due to an annoying ransomware virus that left you with blue skin unless you paid up. And then the feds shut down the company running the ransomware scheme, making the pay-for-cure service unavailable anyway, so those who were turned blue by the encrypted code were stuck that way permanently. Still, those who assumed that she was related to one of the most influential senior engineers in the company treated her with respect, so that was a bonus.

The plan was to manage the wavefield and initiate the jump remotely, using a specific radar frequency as a waveguide, in order to initiate a signal lock.

* * *

This was only half of the puzzle. The system was entirely dependent on quantum communication via entangled bit-pairs and thus, one of the qubits had to be sent forward in order for the system to work—there was no possibility of sending anything "back" until the forward link had already been established.

This, of course, ruled out sending anything back to a time period before the Qmunications technology had been invented. Thus, the initial plan was to use the existing equipment and field generation equipment at the Novelty Hill facility, but the folks at Cornerstone had a different idea.

As it turned out, way back in 1947, the AAF (Army Air Forces) had set up the first postwar general surveillance radar organization under the direction of the Air Defense Command at McChord on the twenty-first day of May, 1947. In addition to the new org's 'general surveillance' mandate, there had also been a top-secret division working under the direction of General Carl Spaatz and his chief scientific advisor, Dr. Theodore von Karman, on remote sensing technology that later became known as "quantum radar." This tech used a set of multidimensional field theory equations that (again, later) became known as four-dimensional wall-crossing.

The 20th century AAF researchers were sending the right kind of quantum signal forward in time in May 1947. They just didn't know it—and they didn't have the right receiving equipment to make the quantum connection. But the scientists at Andna, 487 years in the future, realized they could use this tech to communicate with the physicists studying this very specific wavefield in the past.

Back in '47, Spaatz and the head of Air Proving Ground Command, Maj. Gen. Carl A. Brandt, had managed to conceal the costs of the top-secret Cornerstone program by burying them in the development budget of the new air defense system—with its much talked-about concept of 'minimum air defense'—that Spaatz was sure the senate would approve. It would cost the United States enormous sums of money, Brandt warned the senate, for equipment, construction, and manpower. The $300 million worth of funding for top-secret quantum radar facilities, equipment, and personnel ensured that it did.

Fortunately, the experiments by the scientists and engineers in 1947 were rigorously documented, with exact times, dates, frequencies, energy levels and all other pertinent field data. The 25th-century team just had to modulate the field in such a way that it would be noticed by a group of 20th-century scientists who almost certainly weren't expecting to find a coded message from the future perturbing their data stream.

But they did. On May 21, 1947, an ionospheric disturbance was recorded by the equipment set up at the nearby McChord base in Washington. The signal sent from the radar tower on Mount Rainier the future had successfully locked on to the carrier wave broadcast from the McChord base. The signal lock only lasted for a few seconds, but it was enough for that first test to be declared a success.

"Signal lock established," reported Leonid.

"Initiate sequence EM1," said Li Yan.

"Sending now...."

Above the radar tower on the mountain, a series of faint, almost rainbow-like ionospheric illuminations lit up the surrounding clouds. They looked like notes resonating on a celestial harp—divine music of the spheres plucked from the heavens and carried earthward by a luminous string.

The team in 2434 had coded their experimental message in a format they felt was sure to be recognized by the military technicians in 1947. Fortunately, their hunch was correct. The technician heard the repeating pattern and realized that it was Morse code. He decoded the message and showed his bewildered commanding officer the decoded result.

"A B C 1 2 3 A B C 1 2 3. Your U.S. Government Top Secret program authorization code is AAF-MC-QRT. Please respond."

Six hours later, a message came back.

"We're getting something," reported Leonid.

.-- .... --- / .. ... / - ....-..

Li Yan and Karl ran over and examined the data. The reply was in Morse code. When decoded, it said *Who is this?*

They understood!

The team in 2434 sent a reply they hoped would allay any fears that the system had been hacked or otherwise compromised by foreign powers.

"This message is from U.S. government scientists working with Air Defense Command at Arlington in the year 2434. Here is proof: On May 22, the Corporal-E ballistic missile will have its first successful test flight and President Truman will sign the Truman Doctrine. Stay tuned. Further information to follow."

There was rejoicing by the folks on both ends of the comms link. The Cornerstone people on the 25th century end of the link realized that they might have just bestowed a great gift upon 1940s America: a 400-year head start into the information age and a huge strategic advantage over the communists. And if they could actually send equipment back, well, the military possibilities were nearly unlimited. They just had to get it working.

The news of this success quickly made its way up the chain of command and, the word was, all the way to President Harry S. Truman, who would indeed sign the document that became known as the Truman Doctrine the next day. It was only then that they were informed by high-ranking intelligence officials about the meaning of the 'Corporal' message. A man who identified himself as a member of the White House security office confirmed that the USA's first guided ballistic missile, the 45-foot-long MGM-5 Corporal, had indeed had its first successful test firing that very morning.

An order came down from the oval office later that afternoon that the project was now designated Top Secret "LIMDIS," limiting distribution only to those specially approved by executive order. It was the date many called "the formal beginning of the cold war."

* * *

2

Sunrise

The next day, top-ranking officials from the CIA, the FBI, the White House security office, and the Joint Chiefs of Staff, gathered in Washington D.C. for an emergency meeting with President Truman in the war room. With them was General Carl Spaatz, telephoning in on a secure line from an undisclosed location.

Spaatz was deeply concerned about the security risks posed by any exposure to information from unverified sources. He was already pushing the Joint Chiefs of Staff for changes to the National Security Act, which in his view was already so weak that the Secretary of Defense could not do his job properly. "The prospect of Russian intelligence planting false information to study U.S. responses is simply unacceptable," he argued.

The president thanked him for his service to the country and continued around the table, gathering insights and opinions from the others in attendance.

It didn't take long for the group to arrive at the consensus that it was possible—indeed, quite plausible—that these prognostications were not from the future at all, but were somehow the work of moles operating within the ranks of the organizations responsible for the missile launch and the signing of the Truman Doctrine—possibly cunning spies or disinformation agents hoping to manipulate foreign policy by following a few accurate disclosures with damaging falsehoods. The Truman Doctrine, the President observed, had been widely discussed since its public announcement in March. It wasn't much of a secret to reveal. And any number of people from the U.S. Army Ordnance California Institute Technology (ORDCIT) or any of its major contractors could have been responsible for leaking information about an upcoming missile test date.

These, the Chiefs of Staff argued, were simply not credible examples of proof that the people from the future were calling. It was agreed that more substantial proof was needed.

The director of the Security Office, however, raised a concern that changed the course of the discussion, if not history itself.

"No matter where this information is from," he began, "I

am concerned that by acting upon it in any way, we would be changing the natural course of history. I recommend that we confer with our leading theoretical physicists to determine what, if any, effect, this might have upon the natural flow of cause and effect. To do otherwise seems to me a fool's errand."

"I agree," said President Truman. The prudent course of action is to understand as much as we can about this topic we currently know so very little about."

At the next meeting, on Thursday, June 5, theoretical physicist Hans Bethe joined them on the phone.

"I have just returned from a most enlightening conference in New York," Bethe proclaimed, "and I remind you that all systems change dynamically in time. Knowing the wave function at one instant is in principle sufficient to calculate it for all future times, however, wave functions can also change discontinuously and stochastically during a measurement. The wave function changes because new information is available. And that, gentlemen, seems to be precisely the situation we have here. We can calculate the probabilities for the different possibilities using the Born rule. But we cannot say they will or will not occur."

"Dr. Bethe, could you phrase that in a simple way for my benefit?" enquired the president. "What are the risks? Should we do this or not?"

Putting it as simply as he could, Bethe said that "the concern is that even the action of gathering new information using a quantum channel is sufficient to alter the wave state and thus risk change to the outcome."

Roscoe Hillenkoetter, the newly appointed head of the

CIA rolled his eyes. "With all due respect, Doctor, I must object. If this message is indeed from Americans reaching out to us from the year 2434, we would have access to roughly 400 years' worth of vital intel on foreign and domestic activities across all walks of life. I think we can all imagine what would happen if our opponents had this kind of information and used it against us. Frankly, I find the possibility of that an unacceptable risk. If this information is available to us, we would be fools not to take full advantage of it."

"But that's just the problem," countered Bethe. "How do you know that you are being contacted by Americans? We've all seen the levels of deception our enemies are willing to stoop to in order to gain an advantage. I would prefer to see the United States take the viewpoint that, if this contact has indeed been initiated from Americans in the year 2434, we can at least be sure of two things: First, that America still exists as a leading scientific and political force at that time, and secondly, that this undeniably strong advantage has grown from our research here and now in microwave radar. These are, I think, perfectly good reasons to assume that the future of America is already playing out as we would wish in a best-case scenario.

"Taking no action at all presumably assures us this possible future. Taking any actions to alter it puts that best-case future at risk. It's as simple as that."

Hillenkoetter scowled but said nothing as the president nodded thoughtfully.

The president declared a moratorium on any actions or documentation pertaining to the capture or decoding of new information until the risks were better understood and quantified. "General Spaatz," he said, "your radar team's instructions for now are to continue with the quantum radar tests, according to the original plan, exactly as they had been doing before the contact was made."

"Understood, sir."

* * *

The team in the 25th century was mystified when, in January 2435, all responses from the radar team in 1947—including automated acknowledgements that acted as 'read receipts' —suddenly ended. At first, they assumed it must be a technical issue. Later, however, they concluded that this might be a security issue. They decided to continue sending data anyway, while they worked toward their aspirational goal: to replicate the HELX time-displacement effect using the multi-D markers and quantum radar fields being broadcast by the 1947 radar researchers.

* * *

The next MDM test took place on January 10, 2435. A highly reflective test object was placed upon the jump platform at Novelty Hill and the wave generation sequence was remotely initiated by Karl, operating the controls from the makeshift control center at Sunrise.

Unfortunately, the signal multiplexer was miscalibrated and eight "ghost images" appeared behind the test object and the nine spectral shapes appeared over the town of Sunrise on June 24, 1947 and hung in the sky long enough to be observed, but failed to materialize.

The teams at both Sunrise and Novelty Hill were aware that the materialization phase had not completed successfully, and they attempted to recalibrate. This caused the ghostly objects to lose their positional sync, and the objects suddenly began moving eastward (or more precisely, southeast, due to the miscalibration) at the rotational speed of the earth: roughly 1000 miles per hour. Despite these issues, the test was considered a qualified success. Even the *illusion* of a fleet of aircraft flying through the skies was considered a military advantage.

* * *

A second test, held ten days later, yielded similar results, due to the same as-yet unresolved calibration issue. The radar teams in 1947 tracked the phantom objects over 400 miles southeast, over southwestern Idaho, following Highway 84 past Nampa, as far away as the then-inactive Mountain Home Army Air Field Base. At that point, the 2435 source team ended the experiment and MHAFB—which was pretty much right underneath the flight path—reported that the radar signal had been lost. Still interesting, but not much of an improvement.

It had been a long day and, although most of the team left to be with their families for dinner on Independence Day, Karl was determined to find the calibration problem and fix it.

After almost two hours of scrutiny, he found the code containing a critical error: an erroneous eight-bit offset was causing the ghosting problem and the multiple images. Exhausted but elated, he ran the initialization routine to test the fix. Too late, he realized he hadn't checked in with the Novelty Hill technicians to let them know he was running the routine again.

* * *

Foreboding thunderheads loomed over Mt. Rainier in the distance as winds swept across the grassy fields of eastern Washington. A sudden change in the wind's direction beneath the darkening sky sent ripples dancing across the field and a trio of cows looked up, their dark eyes suddenly illuminated by a flickering blue light. Startled, two of the cows recoiled in alarm as the third was suddenly engulfed in the blue light and dropped lifeless to the ground. Lightning crackled overhead as a flock of startled birds scattered in flight and, not far away, a fox scurried for shelter. In the middle of the field, a translucent curtain of blue and white undulated as it extended into the clouds above the grassy landscape. The intensity of the light faded as it neared the ground, where it flickered and danced over a mutilated carcass. It then abruptly moved to a different location, then another and another, all in a straight line. This flickering curtain of light continued to flash on and off intermittently at different locations along a straight line extended toward the horizon. The speed of the flashes increased until it became a flickering line with a single bright area. The flickering effect diminished, leaving a bright section that then began moving—slowly at first, then gradually gaining speed as it moved like a wave, ever more rapidly towards the distant clouds to the southeast.

A few seconds later, it had disappeared over the horizon.

****

Seconds later, the communications panel lit up green. The transmission had succeeded.

A moment later came the call with the bad news: there had been two technicians and several diagnostic modules on the pad when it disappeared, along with them.

In the executive office, Kroeger picked up the phone. It was someone from the lab.

As he listened, his eyes widened and his jaw grew tense. "How did this happen?" he said at last.

He listened intently for a moment, as the scenario was described.

"He what?!" Kroeger took a deep breath. "Just a moment." He punched a button on the intercom. "Cancel my appointments."

"Yessir," said his receptionist.

"And get Karl Schraeder from the lab up here, *asap*."

A few minutes later, the intercom buzzed. "Mr. Schraeder is here," said Kroeger's executive assistant.

"Send him in."

Kroeger gestured to a chair as Karl entered the room. "Hello Karl, sit down." As Karl slid uneasily into the leather chair on the opposite side of the desk, Kroeger got right to the point. "So, I understand there's been some trouble in the lab, *hm*?"

"Yessir, and I take full responsibility," said Karl resolutely. "I solved a big problem that we've been having—you know, the calibration issue that was causing the unsuccessful transmissions—and I accidentally ran the initialization routine while testing it. Unfortunately, two staff members and some pieces of equipment were on the platform when the transmission occurred."

"Hm. I see. What's the status of these two individuals?"

"That's unknown, sir. Unfortunately, both the Qmunications transmitter and receiver were on the platform at the time of transmission, so we've temporarily lost the ability to communicate with the folks back there at McChord."

"Yes, that is unfortunate. What's the plan for rectifying the situation?"

"We're still working on that, sir. The current thinking is that we will need to make some repairs and replace the equipment that was lost before we can proceed with re-establishing communications. Once the repairs are complete, we'll have to configure a new receiver module and get it linked to the Qmunications transmitter. We should then then be able to continue with our original objective."

"Do we have a timeline for these repairs yet? How long until we're back up and running?"

"No sir, we're still reviewing the situation down there. Because the transit module was not on the pad at the time of the accidental transmission, we suffered some collateral damage to the controllers, the structural panels, and the diagnostic modules that were on and adjacent to the platform. Until we get those replaced, we won't be able to let them know what's happened."

"Obviously, getting that equipment working is a key priority. Put extra people on that and get me a date asap when we can expect to be operational again. And keep me informed of any snags. That's all for now."

As he left the office, Karl breathed a sigh of relief. That had gone much better than expected.

Kroeger picked up the phone and punched the intercom button. "Get me someone at Cornerstone."

* * *

"Bradley Jackson from Cornerstone on line one."

Kroeger picked up the phone. "Thanks for getting back to us. Look, there's been an accident at the lab. We're assessing the impact, but I just wanted to give you guys a heads-up on this.

"Looks like a kind of a good news-slash-bad news situation. Apparently, the operational error that we were experiencing was a calibration issue that we managed to resolve. However, due to what seems to be human error, the testing of the fix did not go as planned and, well, a couple of staff members are currently unaccounted for. No, no—*our* staff. There's certainly a good chance that we will know more once we get the communications system back up and running. And of course, we'll need to have a full review of exactly what occurred, what went wrong, and what we need to do to make sure this sort of thing doesn't happen again."

"What exactly does 'unaccounted for' mean? Are they alive?"

"Well, that's still a question mark, until we re-establish communications. But we have every reason to believe that the transmission was successful, so there's a very good chance that they might be A-OK."

"I'm going to need to give a status report to the folks in the oval office. Where are we at with the planned intelligence briefings? Are those impacted as well?"

"I'm afraid so. All comms are completely down at the moment, and I don't have an estimate for a restart date yet."

"You'd better get one pretty damn fast."

"I know. I've ordered the staff in the lab to put extra resources on the problem and they're working on it as quickly as possible. It's priority one. I'll certainly keep you informed."

"See that you do. You need to get this shitstorm under control immediately."

"Yes, I will. Good day." The phone connection had already gone dead by the time he finished the sentence.

* * *

3 |

Corona

One hour later

St Augustin Plains, 26 miles southeast of Corona, NM
Friday, July 4, 1947; 10:30 p.m.

As lightning flashed in the darkness, a Gila monster suddenly raised its head. It scuttled across the dark New Mexico landscape toward a rocky embankment. The brief illuminations provided momentary views of cacti and wild brush beneath a stormy sky. As the lightning flickered in the distance, the eyes of a small fox flashed red as it caught another flickering reddish light from an unseen but much closer source. The fox darted away, startled. Suddenly, BOOM!

An object moving at terrific speed traversed the field, close to the ground. Bright red and purple fringes on the shadowy object's perimeter edges flared conspicuously around an otherwise invisible object as it rose higher into the air and banked. An enormous roar split the silence of the desert night.

Shadows cast from the cacti by the fast-moving craft panned rapidly across the desert surface as the object screamed past, close to the ground and kicking up dust. In hot pursuit was a 1940s-era F-86D Sabre interceptor jet aircraft, afterburners ablaze. The plane banked sharply left, then right as its pilot chased the glowing outline through the swirling dust-clouds. Both were moving at high speed as the plane pursued the red and purple fringes of light.

The mysterious object banked at a terrific speed, close to the ground, as the plane struggled to keep up.

22 miles away, a military air traffic controller tracked the object and its pursuer on a radar screen. "Alpha Tango One, reduce your speed. Target is 15 degrees north-northwest from your present position and slowing down. 900 miles per hour ... 500 ... now 150 miles per hour. It's slowing down. Intercept in 7 seconds."

A different voice crackled over the radio. "Alpha Tango One, do not engage. I repeat, do not engage."

"Roger that."

The pilot of AT-1 banked the jet sharply eastward and the jet circled around a hovering disk-shaped object, like a flattened hat with what resembled a fence around its brim. The dust—or was it mist? —lit up a cloud-bank overhead, as flickering lights emanated from slat-like vertical openings in its side panels. Its underside glowed as if by unseen lights.

A few miles away, Frank Harding, owner of Harding Hardware, was just leaving the movie house with his wife Nora after a double-feature screening of *The Hat Box Mystery* and *The Woman on the Beach*. Nora straightened the shoulders of her light sweater by the flickering light of the neon movie marquee as Frank rustled in the jacket pocket slung over his left arm for his car keys.

It was just after 10:30 p.m., outside the Plains Theatre on Main Street. The late-night movie feature was over and other couples filed out of the brass-handled doors beneath the names on the brightly lit marquee.

A middle-aged man tipped his hat to the woman, then pulled the unlit cigarette from his mouth and spoke. "Hello Nora, Frank. Hey Frank. Are you open tomorrow?"

"Sure thing, Bud. 9 a.m. sharp."

"All right. See you then. G'night, you two. Happy Fourth."

The young man and woman crossed the street and walked to the dark green Plymouth closest to the corner. He unlocked the passenger-side car door and opened it for her. She put her purse onto the seat beside her and slid across to open his door. He shut the driver-side door and smiled at her, then opened the no-draft window and turned the key in the ignition. He pulled the big stem-shifter into first gear and turned on the lights. He eased his foot off the clutch and swung the big car smoothly onto Main Street, in the opposite direction from most of the other traffic.

"Shall we take the scenic route home?"

Nora smiled, sizing up the weather. "Sure, Frank. Looks like it might rain, though."

As the car left the well-lit downtown streets and headed onto the road out of town, the number of lamp posts diminished until it just car headlights and cacti as they cruised along beneath the stormy sky.

"So," he asked her, "did you like the movie?"

"Which one? The short one? Nah. That thing was over in 45 minutes flat. That barely qualifies as a feature film."

"No, the second one."

"Well, he should have married the blonde, obviously. But

the nice guys never do, do they? That leading man reminds me a bit of you, you know, with that lovely voice of his."

"Yes, I'm always having mad dreams about ghostly blondes, while completely infatuated with a wicked married woman."

"Oh really? A mysterious brunette?"

"Well, he is completely mad."

"He's not mad, he's just war-torn."

"Well," he teased, turning on the car's interior light. "Let's have a look at you. Ah yes, those big eyelashes look just like—hey, look at that!"

He pointed behind her. From behind a low hill, a weird light pulsed. Flashes of light could be seen as the car sped by.

A low-flying object passed overhead.

"Hey, it's moving!"

Lightning flashes illuminated a strange mist around the bizarre-looking object.

"Wow! What *is* that?"

Frank and Nora peered through the windshield into the direction of the lights as they headed into the darkness. The car's momentum faltered. Frank pressed his foot harder onto the accelerator and the car lurched forward as he turned toward the action at an intersection where a white farmhouse stood.

The farmhouse was briefly illuminated by a nearby lightning flash. Inside, rancher William 'Mack' Brazel and his 14-year-old daughter Bessie were in the living room listening to "*Peg o' My Heart*" by The Harmonicats on their Majestic 4158 radio console, when the radio reception faltered and phased out.

A peal of thunder rattled the window as the annoyed rancher fiddled with the dial. The car's headlights reflected off the glass as it roared past the farmhouse in pursuit of the object.

Inside the car, Frank leaned forward, trying to get a better view. The storm seemed to be almost directly overhead now. Bright lights reflected in the car's chromium trim as lightning struck close to the object and the thunder boomed. The lights underneath it flickered and flashed as the illuminated object careened closer, seemingly out of control. The object rapidly descended, no more than 50 feet from the north side of the road. Frank hit the brakes hard and the car skidded to a halt on the dusty road.

He threw open the driver's side door and jumped out. "Come on!"

Nora had just opened her door when, suddenly, BOOM!

They both ducked involuntarily as a terrific explosion ripped through the night. The startled couple was silhouetted by a cascading ribbon of light and shadow as debris scattered across the landscape.

In the sudden darkness, two bodies were flung violently to the ground amid the wreckage. A cloud of dust rose from the scene of the crash.

Mack and Bessie were startled by the noise. It was so loud, it rattled the farmhouse windows.

"What the Sam Hill...?!" he exclaimed with alarm in his voice.

"Good lord," said Bessie. "That thunder was *loud!*"

"That was no thunder I've ever heard. I think it might've

been a bomb." Mack angrily swiveled his feet to the left and down off the hassock and sat forward in his chair, looking out the window to his left as he turned off the hissing radio. He pushed his feet hurriedly into the slippers next to the hassock, then shuffled over to the cabinet near the door. He grabbed his rifle and a box of shells and opened the door.

As he stepped out onto the porch, Bessie called after him. "You'd better call the sheriff, papa."

"Dangit, can't see nuthin' out there. Get me the flashlight from the drawer in the kitchen, willya, Bess?"

As Bessie ran into the kitchen, Mack re-entered the house and picked up the phone. He finished dialing just as Bessie returned with the flashlight.

The phone rang. Sheriff George Wilcox picked it up on the second ring. "Sheriff's office."

"Hey George. This is Mack Brazel at Foster's ranch."

"Oh, hi Mack. "

"Can you come up here? There's been some sort of explosion just now."

"What's that? What kind of explosion? Like a lightning strike? Or fireworks, maybe?"

"No, not like that. Like an explosion. Like dynamite—a real big boom."

"Are you at the house? Was it something inside the house?"

"No, definitely not. It was outside the house, out in the back field I think."

"Oh, okay. All right, I'll come right over there."

"Yeah, yeah, okay. I'll be here."

"All right."

"Thanks George."

He hung up phone and reached for his hat.

As the thundercloud passed over, a light rain began to fall as Frank and Nora scrambled up the hill for a closer look. As the dust cleared at the scene of the explosion, the lights of the town of Roswell, about 59 miles southeast, twinkled in the distance of the New Mexico nighttime sky. It was eerily quiet. Strangely, there was no crashed ship to be seen. One of the bodies stirred in the darkness.

* * *

4

Recovery

Roswell Army Air Field, New Mexico
Saturday July 5, 5:57 a.m.

Faint streaks of color signaled the break of dawn over the sparse New Mexico landscape. The early morning light was competing with the sodium lamps to cast long shadows and hues alternately pink and yellow across single-storey buildings and 1940s aircraft visible through a high chain-link fence. A guard on early-morning security patrol walked past a sign posted saying Roswell Army Air Field, and another, smaller, sign saying All Visitors Must Register at Main Gate. Beyond this outer perimeter fence, three more armed guards stood near another security gate leading to a large hangar.

A few minutes later, the area was bustling with activity. Two separate groups of military personnel assembled on the east side of the hangar as planes were being pulled out of the hangar and onto the apron by the pushback tractors. A large truck pulled up and parked nearby.

At last, when all of the planes had been moved clear of the area in front of it, the truck backed into the hangar and slowed to a stop.

On the other side of the apron was the Military Command building, where a single office on the second floor was illuminated. Inside, Colonel Samuel Jennings was talking on the phone. Behind him, a clock read 6:04 a.m. On the uncluttered desk in front of the colonel were five slightly curled black and white photos showing aerial views of the craft and, on the table next to the desk, a large map of the Roswell/Corona area, with the coordinates 33.949959, -105.314529 marked in red and a red circle drawn around the crash site.

Jennings was scribbling notes as he held the telephone handset with his other hand. "Yessir, we will sir. At 0630 sharp. Yes, he's here. I understand, sir, thank you." On the other side of the table, Major Jesse A. Marcel studied the map.

Jennings hung up the phone.

"Major Marcel..."

Marcel replied with a dialect borne of his upbringing in Houma, Louisiana. "Yessir?"

"Get all the on-duty five-o-nines in here for a briefing in five minutes. Tell 'em it's pri one. I'm going to need a helicopter and a pilot. And find Colonel Blanchard. I'll be in the briefing room."

"Right away, sir."

* * *

Saturday July 5, 6:45 a.m.

Frank Harding and his wife Nora heard the sound of an approaching helicopter and hid on the shadowy side of the hillock. When they became apparent that it was landing nearby, they peered out from behind a sagebrush bush and saw an amazing sight in the dawn's early light. Bright lights from the overhead helicopter illuminated the site. The area around the crash was completely cordoned off. Military personnel were everywhere. A large number of panel truck-type vehicles were parked in a semicircle near where a tent had been pitched. From their nearby vantage point, Frank Harding and his wife Nora watched through binoculars. They witnessed seven workers in hazmat suits carry debris and what appeared to be bodies to the trucks, as others inspected the ground with Geiger counters and other gear. Some of the debris looked like plastic strips and metallic panels; long strands of wire and broken pieces of building—or flooring?—material were also visible. But there was no "ship" visible.

Frank, handing Nora the binoculars, whispered: "What do you make of that, Nora?"

Nora studied the debris intently. "It looks like some sort of cleanup operation of—*whatever* it is. Some kinda electronic equipment? I can't rightly make it what something like that would be used for out here. It's damn strange, ain't it?"

She handed the binoculars back to Frank.

Frank: "I dunno. I ain' never seen any kit that looks like that, with all them metallic panels 'n wires 'n all. It seems like they's lookin' for radiation or somethin'. And look! That's a body they're putting into that truck." He handed her the binoculars again.

Nora adjusted the binoculars for a clearer look. "Maybe it's one of them flyin' saucer folk?" She focused her attention on untangling the strap of the leather case around her neck. "Dang. Here, you take these." From the case she pulled a small camera.

He took another look.

"It is definitely Army. Five hundred and ninth division, it says. I think that might be Mack Brazel over there by that truck with the Army guy. And that looks like Sheriff Wilcox he's talkin' to! He's not lettin' the sheriff get in there. Ol' George ain' gonna like *that*."

He slid down behind the crest of the hill and turned to Nora. "I think we should tell Randy."

"At the paper?"

Frank lowered the binoculars and nodded vigorously. "Yes."

Nora was taking photos with her Baby Brownie camera.

"I don' know, Frank. What if this is some top-secret thing we're not supposed to be seein'? I am not givin' him this film. I want to see these pictures for myself."

Frank peered over the hilltop one last time. "Come on. It is getting awful busy aroun' here."

They slid down the far side of the hill toward their car—a 1946 Dodge—at the bottom of the hill.

* * *

At the crash site, the workers had almost completed the

cleanup operation. Three of the workers raked the ground with brooms and rakes, covering their tracks all the way back to the trucks. The rear doors of the panel trucks were shut and locked. A moment later, the trucks backed up and turned back toward the road with their headlights off. The vehicles kicked up small trails of dust as they pulled onto Highway 247 and headed east across the Plains of San Augustin in the direction of Roswell Field. Frank and Nora's Dodge turned and headed south toward Lincoln County.

* * *

An hour later, Frank and Nora sat in a booth at the O'Niner Diner with local newspaper editor Randy Hatfield. Behind the counter, Darla the waitress tried to look busy.

Frank rattled the spoon noisily around the cup as he stirred his coffee excitedly. "I'm telling you Randy, we both saw it. I swear on my mother's grave, I think it might have been one o' them flying saucers we've been hearin' about."

Nora was almost as effusive as he was. "We were in the car on the way into town and it jus' flew *right* past, and we followed it up Corona way there best we could. It exploded like a bomb hit it, right by the hill down there at the north end of Foster's ranch. You know, the one Mack Brazel runs now, up toward Corona there."

Darla refilled their cups and Frank poured the last of the cream into his. "I'll getcha some more o' that," she promised.

"We *heard* the explosion. And they started closing off that whole area just after we got there. They were poking around, lookin' for *some*thing. We watched the army clean the whole thing up from up on that little ol' hill. I think they shot some-thin' down, I really do."

Nora watched Randy as he wrote down what Frank had said. "They were all *over* it," she added. "And there was all kinds of *unusual* debris, all shiny wires and weird lookin' metal panels and the like."

Frank was emphatic. "That recovery operation was defi-nitely military," he insisted, "with those 5'o'9 group markings on the trucks. They had Geiger counters and guys in them big white suits an' metal detectors an' *every*thing."

Nora lowered her voice. "And there were bodies. I think they were, you know, dead. Maybe like *War of The Worlds* aliens."

Darla leaned in with the refilled creamer.

Frank, following Nora's cue, suddenly spoke quietly. "An' get this," he practically whispered. "Before they left, they raked over the area to hide all the footprints and impact marks an' all the, you know, *evidence*."

Randy dutifully wrote it all down in his notebook. "You'd better tell George Wilcox," he said. "This is certainly a matter of interest to the police, if there's been injuries or deaths."

Frank put his hand over his coffee as Darla, still struggling to listen in, leaned in to refill the cup. "No thanks, darlin'."

Darla dropped the bill onto the table and headed back behind the counter, where she pretended to be busy as she listened with interest.

Frank was trying his best to be persuasive. "Lookit, we can go right ahead and get Sheriff Wilcox involved if you want to, but it's a little above his pay grade, I'd say. But this is a damn sight bigger story than who the King of Romania is fixin' to marry. I mean, it's such *crap* that passes for news on the radio these days."

Nora opened her purse and slid a dollar onto the table. "We gotta get goin' an' open the store, Randy, but thanks for hearin' us out. Sorry it was so early. You're a dear."

Nora always understood Randy better than Frank did.

Frank shook Randy's hand as they got up to leave. "Look," he shrugged, "this is somethin' big—I just know it."

Frank held the diner door open for Nora and looked back at Randy, who was still scribbling notes on a steno pad. "Say hi to Nancy for us."

As she reached the door, Nora added: "Oh, by the way, tell Nancy that shipment of Stoddard Solvent she ordered came in. See you soon!"

Amid the notes on Randy's notepad, a headline was heavily underlined: *RAAF Captures Flying Saucer on Ranch in Roswell Region*.

* * *

5

Prominence

Roswell Army Air Field, NM.
Saturday July 5, 1947
8:30 a.m.

Most of the rooms in the building on the south side of Roswell Army Air Field were dark. But the lights were on in the second-floor office of Col. William H. Blanchard as his assistant poked her head into the room. "Colonel Jennings is here to see you."

Blanchard was on the phone behind his desk, waiting for a connection. He gestured to her. "I'm on hold. Tell him to come in and sit down. I'll be right with him."

Colonel Samuel Jennings entered the room and sat in the chair beside the desk.

"Thanks for coming down here," said Blanchard, covering the mouthpiece of the phone. "Have you seen these?"

He pushed several slightly curled black and white photos showing aerial views of the crash site, across his cluttered desk. Jennings examined the ones closest to him. Blanchard pointed to a pair of eight-by-tens.

"No, not those ones. These are more detailed. Much better."

"These are from this morning's operation?" Blanchard asked, as he examined them with the magnifying glass on the desk.

"Yes. I'll provide you with copies to take back." The phone clicked and a voice could be heard on the line.

"*Hello?*"

"Just give me a minute to take this call."

He spoke into the phone. "Good morning, General. This is Colonel Blanchard." He fell quiet for a moment as he listened. "I understand, sir, we'll get right on it. Yessir, happy fourth to you too."

"Sorry Sam," Col. Blanchard said as he hung up the phone, "but it seems we've come into possession of quite a hot potato. The general and *his* superior officer are flying back from D.C. on Tuesday to brief us on next steps. The meeting is scheduled right after they land, at 1400 hours. So, we'll need the conference room spic and span before then, okay?"

"Spic and span, sir?"

"It's a cleaner—a detergent. My wife swears by it."

"I see, sir."

"And he's requested reinforcements to the security at the front gate and hangar B. I want three armed guards posted outside the hangar and two more at the gate. And double the watch along the perimeter fence. That'll be all for now."

Jennings picked up his hat and stood up. "Roger that, Colonel."

Col. Blanchard opened the door for him. Thanks again for coming down here on the holiday weekend."

Sam Jennings tipped his hat to the receptionist and flashed a friendly smile. "No problem, *sir*."

* * *

Sunday, July 6

At the diner, Frank paged through the morning paper with increasing frustration. "What the H-E--? There's no damn coverage of it at all."

He folded the paper roughly and slammed it down on the table. "Damn!"

Nora regarded the frowning faces now looking at them and spoke sternly under her breath. "Frank—you hush up now. Come on. Maybe it's jus' the holiday schedule getting in the way. You jus' know Randy's wasn't s'pose to be workin' yesterday, nor today neither. Come on, I'm sure it will be there tomorrow."

Frank was not convinced. "I'm callin' the dang radio station again. And George Wilcox, too."

That night, the silence was shattered as a brick was thrown through the glass window of Harding Hardware. A note was affixed to it with a red rubber band. On the note was written a single word: TRAITOR.

* * *

Monday, July 7

The bell above the door of Harding Hardware tinkled as a woman entered the store. As she entered, she passed the boarded-up window. She was the only customer in the store. In the background, a radio played *Civilization* by the Andrews Sisters with Danny Kaye at a low volume.

Nora stood her broom in the corner and tapped the dustpan into the garbage bin behind the counter. "Well, Nancy, what a pleasant surprise. How's Davy?"

Nancy smiled and glanced at the clock the wall. "Oh, he's fine, jus' fine. Listen, I, ah, jus' came in to um, pay for that solvent I ordered. You got that in, right?"

"Oh yeah, we got five or six cans back there. But Frank'll deliver that. They are too heavy to carry far."

Nancy looked distracted. "Yeah, sure. Tha' sounds real good. Listen, uh, Nora. Is Frank around?"

"Oh sure, he's in the back, I expect." She smiled. "I think he's got the radio on back there."

Nora peered at Nancy, the worry showing through her fading smile. "Do you *want* me to get 'im?"

Nancy shook her head. "No, no, it's okay. Actually, I jus' wanted a quick word with you. About what you told Randy about—you, know, what you said you *saw*?"

Nora's eyes narrowed slightly. "Mm *Hmm...*"

Nancy shuffled awkwardly. "Well, Randy, he, ah, wasn't going to run that particular story, you know. Nothin' personal, but it sounded so, you know, *incredible*. But then..."

Nancy breathed deeply and looked around nervously as a man walked by, just outside the store window.

"There were others. We received *two* anonymous notes and

then... we got a call from ol' Mack him*self*, wantin' to know what the heck's goin' on—he felt like all these strangers pokin' around on his ranch land were not telling him the truth, you know? And then, all these planes flying around down there since then. So, needless to say, the story's become a little more interesting, you might say."

Nora looked mildly exasperated. "Well, Nancy, I know what I saw. So, are you saying that Randy now sees this news as fit to print in the *Daily Record*?"

Nancy nodded her head. "Oh, it *will* run. It's front-page news, the biggest headline in tomorrow's paper. I've seen the layout. We got those plates all ready to run. He was workin' on it all weekend. It's a big story. And what's-her-name, Judy from the radio station, she was asking folks *at church* about it, too. Can you be*lieve* that? They called us about the story, too. And *then....*"

She pursed her lips for a second before continuing.

"They started talkin' about it on the 9 o'clock news. Last night. I know, I know. That's unbelievable, right? And then, I swear *right in the middle* of the broadcast, they *cut off* the story! Like 'Whoops, we ain' supposed to talk about *that*.' Now *every*body's talkin' about it. So, how much do I owe you for the solvent?"

Nora did the calculation in her head, as she usually did. "five twenty-five a can. That's uh, thirty-one fifty for all six. And, of course, that's for manufacturing, so there's no tax on that."

Nancy pulled out her checkbook and fished about in her purse for a pen. "Okay, here ya go."

"I'll get Frank to drop off the receipt with the cans. Prob'ly half pas' five or so. Will that be all right?"

"Sounds perfect. Thanks, Nan."

Nancy closed her purse and snapped it shut. "So, what did the ... *aliens* look like?"

Nora shrugged. "Honestly, Nan, I didn't get a real good look. Frank was hoggin' the binoculars a bit. But they had 'em on stretchers. And they took 'em away. Down to the base, I 'spect. I heard from Mack's boy that they were there— no lie—three whole days. Doin' exactly what, I can hardly imagine."

* * *

Tuesday, July 8

6:58 a.m.

The radio at the diner was playing *"Rumors Are Flying"* by Frankie Carle.

Frank set down his coffee cup with satisfaction and tapped his finger on the lead story in the morning paper. "Now *that's* more like it. Lookit, Nora, that'd be you mentioned right there on page 1. How 'bout that, huh?"

Two cowboy types walked by their booth. One slapped Frank playfully on the shoulder with a folded-up newspaper. "Woo, look at you, Frank. The hardware man finds the *aliens*. Howdy, Nora."

The other, a younger man, tipped his Stetson. "M'am."

Behind the counter, Darla suddenly turned up the radio.

"... special report from KSWS Roswell Radio News."

"Hey, listen to this."

"The intelligence office of the 509th Bombardment group at the Roswell Army Airfield announced today that the field has come into possession of a flying saucer. According to information released by the department, over …"

The remainder of the broadcast was mostly inaudible due to the increasing volume of the whoops and shouts of the patrons of the diner.

"Quiet, ya'll," Darla hissed. "We're tryin' t' listen here."

"… authority of Major J. A. Marcel, intelligence officer, the disk was recovered on a ranch in the Roswell vicinity, after an unidentified rancher notified Sheriff George Wilcox that he had found the …"

"Unidentified?!" exclaimed Frank. "Hmph! You just *know* that means it was old busybody Brazel."

Darla turned the radio back down when the special report ended. "Wow, this is huge, Frank. You and Nora could be real celebri*ties*."

Chef Marco opened the door to the kitchen and yelled in Frank's direction: "Hey, *hey,* who do we know down at the base there?"

Frank counted on his fingers. "They prob'ly won' talk, but Jimmy Jones, he's there, and Bill, um, Bill Mebbleson, he and his dad are both there. So those three, I guess."

In the next booth, old James and Edna Frobisher were having their usual Tuesday breakfast.

James leaned over toward the side of the booth where Frank sat and spoke quietly. "His dad won' talk. But Billy might."

Edna chimed in from the other side of the table: "You

should come to church more often, you two. *Every*body was talkin' bout it there, and next Sunday, I expect, will take that to a whole other level. And Frank, you need to set a few people *straight*."

6

Pink and Blue

July 8, 0900 hours
Military Command Conference Room A

Several officers, including Major Jesse Marcel, Colonel Payne Jennings Jr, CIC Agent Sheridan Cavitt and Colonel William Blanchard sat around a large wooden table.

Blanchard moved to the podium and addressed the officers in the room. "Gentlemen, we have been ordered to manage the flow of information regarding the 'Corona Incident' both outside and within the base. In order to do that, it is imperative that no further information be disclosed or otherwise revealed about the *alleged* flying disk now in our possession, by the order of the Intelligence Office.

"Instead, we are going to provide an alternative narrative making it crystal clear that no such event has occurred."

"But sir," protested Jesse Marcel. "We'll have to say *something.*"

"Oh, we will," the colonel assured him. "Our position is that that this was a case of simple misidentification. The specific details are still being worked on, but we'll get there."

"Major Marcel, as this was your op, please coordinate with Public Information Officer Walter Haut, to see that an appropriate press release makes its way to local radio stations KGFL and KSWS, the *Morning Dispatch* and *Daily Record* newspapers and any other members of the media who come around asking for information no sooner than 13 hundred hours today, at which time you may also release the information through our internal communications channels as well.

"I will be heading out at 10 hundred hours to personally meet with Governor Mabry in Santa Fe tomorrow afternoon to brief him on the situation. And, as we approach the Army Air Force's 40th anniversary, I will also be requesting that the Governor formally proclaim August 1st as Air Force Day in New Mexico, which I am hopeful will lead to some good things for all of us.

"In any event, I expect to be occupied there for at least two weeks, maybe longer. Colonel Jennings will be in charge here during my absence. Any questions?"

The others shook their heads. Marcel was the only one who spoke. "No sir."

Blanchard looked pleased. "That is all. Dismissed. Major Marcel, will you stay behind for a moment, please?"

"What do we know about this thing so far, major? Any idea of where it might have come from?"

Marcel paged through a small blue notebook. "Well, sir,

we've made a few interesting discoveries. Do you have time for a quick tour?"

Blanchard checked his watch. "I've got 10 minutes. Let's go."

* * *

Outside hangar 1B, Blanchard and Marcel approached the armed guards. The guards saluted and handed the men a clipboard to sign. One of the guards spoke into a radio transmitter clipped to his vest. A few seconds later, the huge hangar doors opened and the two men entered.

Inside, the hangar was bustling with activity. The officers walked by several workers operating various pieces of equipment, and there were carts with additional equipment everywhere.

In front of them, on an elevated series of metallic platforms supported and steadied by a framework of steel cables and girders, sat a collection of partially reassembled parts and pieces that looked nothing like an alien flying saucer. If anything, it looked more like a room from *inside* a spaceship. A circular perimeter wall was mostly intact, but with about a third of its disc-shaped floor broken and missing. A smaller cylindrical area protruding from the underside sported what appeared to be doors or access panels, some of which were open or missing.

Blanchard pondered the scene for a moment before speaking. "That is some weather balloon. Is there more?"

Marcel shook his head, "Nope, this is it."

Blanchard looked puzzled. "Strange ... and what about the flight crew?"

Marcel referred to his notes. "We have one in serious condition and one pronounced dead at the scene. We believe that's all accounted for, sir. The live one is in an isolation room in medical building 4B. The other one is on ice in 4C, which we've sorta turned into a makeshift containment lab. The docs think it was just injuries from the crash that killed it."

Blanchard raised an eyebrow. "Was it a him or a her, Major?"

Marcel looked slightly bemused. "Well, the doc has been poking around a bit and the dead one is apparently a male—fair hair and pale complexion, but they're kinda different. No belly button. And the live one is very strange, too. She's *blue*."

Blanchard looked genuinely surprised. "So, the males are pink and the females are blue? Hm."

"It would appear so, sir."

"But just about as fragile as we are in a crash-landing, it would seem."

Marcel nodded. "It would indeed, sir."

Blanchard put his hands together behind his back as he walked. "That *is* good to know. All right. What do we know about where this unusual ship came from?"

"Let me find someone who can brief you on that, sir." Marcel approached one of the workers. "Private, who's in charge here this morning?"

"That would be Sgt. Marston, right over there. Hey Sarge!"

Marston approached and saluted each of the officers in turn. "Sir. Sir."

"Sergeant, as you know, Major General Clements Mc-Mullen in Washington has expressed considerable interest in our operation here and there's a good chance he may want to move the project to higher ground. What have we learned so far?"

"Well, we have a fairly complete set of measurements at this point: circumference, weight, volume, material thicknesses and so on, and we're just working out the layout of where we think all the pieces belong. It's a bit of a puzzle. We're thinking that maybe the bottom fell out of the ship or was ejected somehow. These materials all seem to be interior surfaces."

"That is puzzling. Anything else?"

"There are many big questions that remain. It seems apparent that the crew breathes oxygen, but we haven't found any evidence of a habitation environment or environmental controls at all. In fact, we really don't know what powers this craft at all. It does not appear to have any kind of engines in there. And it doesn't appear air-tight."

"Which is a little odd, isn't it?"

Blanchard turned to Marcel. "Looks like we didn't find the whole ship. Have Jennings arrange for an aerial sweep along the projected flight path with you onboard. You'll keep your eyes open for possible impact craters or additional debris fields. Get photos if you see anything. There must be some exterior surfaces we haven't found yet. Maybe the craft just grazed the ground when it came down. And you report anything unusual to Jennings."

"Understood, sir."

He turned back toward Sgt. Marston. "So, given that we

don't know much about the environmental requirements of the crew, you'd say that there's a significant risk to the subjects there?"

"Yessir, I would. At this point, we know very little about their biology. However, the forensic report from Dr. Kimball at the lab suggests that their overall physiognomy is very much like ours overall, albeit with that unusual skin pigmentation in one of the subjects. Maybe not human, but close. That report will be in the materials we will be sending over before end of day, sir."

"Sounds good. Thank you, Sergeant, we'll head over there to the lab now. Keep up the good work."

"Thank you, sir."

* * *

Did you know?
In 1947, Lorenzo Kent Kimball was a Captain, U.S. Army (Medical Administrative Corps) assigned to Squadron M (Base Hospital), 509th Bomb Group at Roswell Army Air Base. His primary duty was Medical Supply Officer for the Base Hospital.

* * *

7

Change of Plans

Marcel and Blanchard entered hospital building 4. It was a World War II cantonment type, one-storey, wooden frame structure that nearly everybody called the labs.

An MP guarding the door let them enter after he reviewed their authorizations. In the first lab, the deceased male was prone on a cart, its lower body covered in a sheet. There were visible signs of serious injury to the upper body. A lab technician worked nearby.

This area was connected to the other lab via a hallway. Another MP guarded its door. Through the glass, they saw the uninjured blue female cowering in the corner. Her intense blue eyes watched them intently as they spoke.

"Jesus, that *is* peculiar. What does it eat?"
"Strangely enough sir, we tried a few different things and we found that it *does* seem to like strawberry ice cream."

"Have you tried communicating with it?"

"We're still working on that, sir. It keeps asking 'Where am

I?' but it doesn't seem to understand any of our responses. We've showed it pictures of the planet, the solar system, the galaxy, but we're not seeing much in the way of recognition. It just keeps saying 'no no no.'"

"Seems pretty dumb for a space-traveling alien."

"Well, it can somehow understand most of our words, so there's still some hope. And it doesn't seem to be hostile in the traditional sense—just disoriented. We'll keep working on it."

"You do that. Keep me informed."

"One more thing, sir. With your permission, we were thinking of preparing a set of questions intended to find out where the other portions of their spacecraft are. That seems like an important piece of the puzzle."

"Good idea, yes. I'm sure Washington will be interested in knowing that we're working on that—thank you."

Blanchard checked his wristwatch, then turned again to Marcel. "I think I've seen enough, Major. Thank you. Let's head back."

* * *

The junior officer opened the door of Blanchard's office in the Military Command building just far enough to poke his head into the room. "There's a call for you sir, from Colonel DuBose," he said.

Blanchard was on another line. He acknowledged the junior officer and held up two fingers. In the outer office, the J.O. picked up the handset. "Yes sir, I understand sir. He'll be right with you, sir."

Inside the office, Blanchard finished his call and punched

the lit button on the phone. "Colonel Dubose. William Blanchard. What can I do for you today?" He listened intently for a moment and scribbled down a few notes. "We'll get that taken care of right away, sir. Same to you, sir." He hung up the phone and turned to Jennings and Marcel. "Change of plans. We've been instructed to transfer all materials relating to the wreckage—including the two subjects in building four—to a superordinate team coming in from Wright Field for a transfer by B-29 to the Fort Worth Army Airfield. Colonel, please work *only* with Maj. Marcel and the staff in the containment units to facilitate this transfer. This has been designated *Top Secret.*"

"Roger that," said Jennings.

Blanchard opened the cabinet and pulled out a thick file folder. "Oh, and Jennings: make a record book entry that states that all records related to the 'Corona Incident' were destroyed without authorization by an unknown party."

* * *

The intercom buzzed. "The driver's here, sir."

Blanchard grabbed his hat and the folder from the desk. "Gotta go. Good luck, men. See you in a couple of weeks."

* * *

"*Ain't Nobody Here But Us Chickens*" blared from the radio in the kitchen. Frank covered the telephone mouthpiece with the palm of his hand and yelled from the hallway. "Hey, turn that down, will you?"

He put the receiver back up to his ear. "C'mon George.

You're the county sheriff. You were *talkin'* to them. Surely, they must have told you *some*thing. Isn't that in your job description?"

He hung up, frustrated.

"He *knows* somethin' but he just won't give it up."

Nora leaned out of the kitchen. "Maybe he's not *allowed* to say."

Frank shrugged. "He's actin' weird."

Nora turned the radio back up again.

* * *

July 8, 1400 hours

The same officers in attendance at the last meeting were now accompanied by two clearly high-ranking senior officers, a warrant officer from Washington D.C. named Robert Thomas and Brigadier General Roger Ramey. General Ramey took the podium and addressed the others.

"Gentlemen, we have a plan. Our folks in Washington believe that the Russkies know at least a little bit about our top-secret 'Project Mogul' balloon designed to monitor Soviet nuclear tests. However, we don't have any intelligence suggesting that they have an inkling about this, uh, alien situation and we'd like to keep it that way.

"So, the plan is to put a cover story out there that the general public might plausibly believe—that this flyin' saucer was just a big ol' weather balloon. The thinkin' is that the Russkies will accept that as a cover-up for a top-secret project—which it actually is. But we get *them* to think that the news stories about this craft are actually talkin' about Project Mogul.

Kind of a double fake-out, if you get my drift. We show 'em a few bits that don't belong on a weather balloon, Russian intelligence tells Moscow that it's obviously Mogul, and we keep the Russkies thinking that we're hiding a failed project they don't know we know that they know about. And if they think that Mogul's a failure, well that's all the better."

"Could work, I guess," mumbled Marcel. Jennings, who was sitting beside him, heard him but didn't respond.

General Ramey continued: "So the official story is weather balloon. We'll put together a little show-and-tell for the media. The actual wreckage of the alien craft now in our possession will be moved to Fort Worth for a more detailed analysis under the code name 'Project Corona.' A decision has not yet been made about what to do with our little blue friend and her unlucky companion. I expect to be briefed on that matter later today.

"At 1100 hours today, a specially prepared B-29 Flying Fortress will depart for the headquarters of the 8th Army Air Force at Fort Worth with the Project Corona wreckage, recovery site data, and all related records and materials. These materials, as you know, are all designated Top Secret.

"Internally, we want you to tell your soldiers that it was just something from a project at Alamogordo, and I want *only* the original nine members of the 5-o-9 recovery team and their immediate officers to have any further involvement, period. We have to lock this thing down *tight*. At approximately 1400 hours, I am holding a press conference at the base at Fort Worth, at which time I will disclose..."

Fort Worth, TX Press Conference
8th Air Force HQ, Carswell Army Air Field
Major Jesse Marcel and Robert Thomas the warrant officer stood next to General Ramey in front of a crowd of newsmen, including J. Bond Johnson of the *Fort Worth Morning Star*.

General Ramey continued: "… the remains of a weather balloon designed to monitor conditions in the upper atmosphere. We subsequently deployed a team to clean up the area and that operation has now concluded without incident."

* * *

July 9
The morning edition of the Roswell Daily Record carried another, smaller, headline about the incident. This time, the story, under the headline "Ramey Empties Roswell Saucer" asserted it was a weather balloon. Another, even smaller headline read "Harassed Rancher Who Located 'Saucer' Sorry He Told About It." Frank was flabbergasted.

"What? What a bunch of … Nora, did you see this?"

An older man in a cowboy hat at the counter turned to face Frank and Nora. "A weather balloon! They are making you look like a fool there, Frank."

"Bah, old Mack Brazel is the fool, if that's what he thinks he saw," said Nora, dismissively.

"It's what they call disinformation, Frank," noted the cowboy's younger companion.

"I believe that's just what it is," remarked a visibly upset Nora. "Come on, Frank."

8

Clampdown

The exhaustive media coverage and subsequent investigation of the widely reported UFO sightings, crash and subsequent recovery caused so much alarm in the President's circle that a strict clampdown was ordered and on July 16, 1947, Congress passed the National Security Act, authorizing the establishment of an independent United States Air Force.

As part of the defense plan, the radar control and warning technology code-named Project SUPREMACY was handed over to Maj. Gen. Francis L. Ankenbrandt. Ankenbrandt's portion of the $600 million budget amounted to $388 million, almost all of which was allocated to the construction and purchase of radar and other equipment.

The military strategists at Project RAND couldn't understand why the government was diverging so much from their offered advice. This was, of course, because only the Joint Chiefs of the War Department, the Office of Scientific Research and Development, the CIA Operations Directorate, and the folks in the Executive Office of the President knew the whole story about the reality behind the UFO stories.

When the whole decoding program was shut down by presidential order, some began to wonder whether the whole thing had been a hoax or whether their department had been shut out of the special access program.

They didn't realize there was another reason the communications from the future had abruptly ceased. It was due to the accident on the jump platform in January 2435. The accident was followed by a lengthy investigation, the preparation and release of a 400-page report, two separate lawsuits and months of hearings about the accident, recommendations and requirements for the design and implementation of new safety standards and the hiring of a new technical director at Andna. Karl Schraeder, it had been decided, had been negligent and had not followed proper procedure. He had to go.

Karl had offered to stay on for a few weeks to help the new technical director get up to speed, but the board wanted him off the project and out of the picture immediately.

Finally, 13 months later, Kroeger approved the resumption of testing.

When the equipment was finally switched back on, the team in February 2436 was disappointed to learn that the read receipts had stopped arriving, along with all other acknowledgements. "Keep sending," suggested Kroeger.

* * *

August 1948
Marcel was called into Blanchard's office. "You're being

transferred to the Strategic Air Command, said the senior Colonel, "where you will be put in charge of a Pentagon briefing session for the Air Force Office of Atomic Energy. Are you up for that, Major?"

Marcel had been hoping for a promotion, but this was unexpected. "Yessir," he said with a smile.

"I'll have a timeline worked out for your transition in a day or two," Blanchard said. "That is all, Major."

* * *

The briefing session was held five days later. Major Jesse Marcel took the podium and addressed the assembled members of the military and scientific communities. "Ladies, gentlemen, please be seated. Thank you. Thank you all for attending this review of our progress to date on the Corona project. As many of you know, we recovered a craft of unknown—possibly extra-terrestrial—origin in July 1947 near Roswell, New Mexico. Since then, our investigations of the craft and its crew have led to some startling discoveries, which have left some big questions unanswered. Before we look at those questions, let's review what we have learned so far."

A slide projector illuminated the screen behind him as Marcel spoke.

The slide said "Defense Department Confidential" in white block letters on a two-tone gray background.

"First," he began, "the craft, which was severely damaged when we found it, appears to be comprised almost entirely of lightweight, super-strong materials of unknown composition. Even some of the more mundane materials recovered from the crash site, such as sections of what would appear to be a simple floor mat, are manufactured of a synthetic material completely unlike any we have seen before. Metallic materials and other conductive elements are composed of unfamiliar alloys, and numerous semi-transparent sheets were found that seemingly fit into a larger overall design—significant portions of which were *not* recovered—composed of some sort of high-density, unbreakable material that remains unfamiliar to our scientists.

"It's not unreasonable to say we have little understanding of how this vessel worked or where it came from. It is, to put it quite bluntly, so advanced that its technology is far beyond our reach.

"One of the most interesting discoveries is what we did *not* find: we've found no evidence of a conventional propulsion system at all. Instead, the craft seemed to function as some sort of multiphase Lorentz Force generator. As near as we can tell, it was capable of generating rotating electromagnetic fields, a little like a multiphase induction motor—but without anything tangibly connected to the motor. Quite frankly, the mechanism by which this thing functions has our scientists baffled.

"We're going to let one of our leading scientists—a researcher by the name of Dr. Hans Bethe—have a crack at it. Apparently, some of the components recovered were not unlike those used to generate and detect quantum fluctuations of an electromagnetic field, which is an area of investigative focus for Dr. Bethe.

"We are slowly but surely learning to communicate with

the visitor, as we call her. There are, however, numerous aspects of their propulsion technology they appear unwilling to share... and their method of reproduction remains a puzzle we barely understand. Our lab has prepared a short film that highlights some of the key progress we have made since last summer."

An assistant started up a 16mm projector and began showing a black and white silent film. It showed the female sitting at a table across from a researcher. The researcher raised a hand and the female matched the hand movement. The researcher then proceeded to demonstrate that the visitor could understand and correctly answer various arithmetic and mathematical problems.

"Clearly," said Jesse Marcel, "the universal language of mathematics is something they are familiar with. We have had less success in understanding her attempts at explaining some of the written language found in the wreckage, which our experts tell me contains iconography that is similar, at least in superficial ways, to ancient Egyptian hieroglyphics."

The film showed closeups of several of the icons found on the equipment recovered from the wreckage.

"As a result of this research, we now have a basic vocabulary by which we can begin to communicate on technological topics with our visitor, who apparently goes by the name 'Frigg.'

"Unfortunately, our visitor has so far been unwilling to explain her purpose in being here or where the other reported craft went—although I wish to emphasize that there is absolutely no evidence to support the idea that they had any hostile intent, or have ties with any foreign government.

"Understanding the technology behind the craft we recovered has been one of the key thrusts of our research. I am told that efforts to reconstruct the craft have been challenging indeed, although some progress *is* being made and we expect to have more information about that real soon.

"As we gain their trust, it is our hope that they will continue to share their technologies and insights with us. To that end, I have been informed that a special research facility, code-named Paradise Ranch, is now under construction on—and underneath—land adjacent to the currently deactivated Las Vegas Army Airfield at Groom Lake, Nevada. When the facility is ready sometime around the end of Q3, we will move the deceased body into cold storage there and continue our investigation of the visitor in a more appropriate and properly equipped high security facility.

"And that is all I have for you today, ladies and gentlemen."

* * *

Did you know?

These developments at Paradise Ranch led to rumors of

engineering based on alien technology, including claims of time travel and teleportation technologies.

* * *

To celebrate Jesse's promotion, he and his wife Janie drove down to Carlsbad on Saturday evening to see a movie at the recently opened Fiesta Drive-in Movie Theater. The film starred Olivia de Havilland as an inmate institutionalized after a breakdown.

After they parked the car, Jesse headed to the concession stand. The feature was just starting when he returned to the car with popcorn and a soda for Janie.

"It was strange," de Havilland's character said. "Here I was among all those people, and at the same time, I felt as if I were looking at them from someplace far away. The whole place seemed to me like a deep hole, and the people down in it like strange animals, like, like snakes, and I'd been thrown into it, yes, as though, as though I were in a snake pit."

With insomnia, memory loss, and mood swings, the confused and frightened inmate couldn't remember the circumstances of her incarceration.

"I can't be sure of anything anymore."

As Jesse watched the scene, he couldn't but think of poor Frigg: confused, frightened and incarcerated, like de Havilland's character.

* * *

Frigg wasn't eating her meatballs. Offerings of strawberry ice cream melted, untouched. She declined to participate in both of her biweekly sessions and seemed increasingly miserable. Earlier in the week, the doctors tried injecting her with 75 mg of chlorpromazine, but it didn't seem to help. Each day, she seemed more and more sullen and withdrawn. There she sat in the corner, with 317 scratch marks on the wall beside her.

The guard unbolted the hatch and slid a plate of food into the cell. Frigg was waiting by the door. She took a bite and fell to the ground, choking. Her arms and legs flailed and then were still.

It didn't take long. The guard called for help and unlocked the door. As he entered the room, she scissor-kicked his feet from under him and he fell loudly onto the ground. She scrambled to her feet and managed to jump over him and make it out of the cell and into the hall. Thomas, the guard who was often friendly to her, ran around the corner and blocked her path forward. "Stop or I'll shoot!" he yelled, but she did not heed the warning. She reversed direction and made it to the stairwell. He ran after her as she threw open the door and ran down the stairs to the main floor.

She ran out of the building and around the corner of the building toward the fence. She attempted to climb the electrified fence but got stuck on the barbed wire.

* * *

Did you know?
[REDACTED] died during an escape attempt November 13, 1953.

9 |

Looking Glass

Sept 28, 2018

The major general checked his watch as he stood at the front of the assembled group of analysts and advisors.

"All right, let's begin," he said. "Welcome and thank you for attending this presentation. Our agenda today is to review the progress made since the visitors and their vessel were first encountered and recovered in July 1947."

He pressed a button on his presentation controller and a progress-to-date summary appeared on the screen behind him.

"Since then, we have worked with medical and scientific experts on two large-scale projects:

- A genomics preservation and propagation effort, which has been quite successful to date.
- A technology stewardship project formerly code-named Corona and now known as Project Looking Glass."

He flipped to the next slide. "For the benefit of those you unfamiliar with Looking Glass, here is a quick overview:

Although it was not understood at the time, it is now clear that many of the then-mysterious properties of some of the materials recovered from the wreckage are now better understood. The shape-memory exhibited by some of the metallic components was subsequently shown to be a well-understood property of the nickel-titanium alloy we now call Nitinol. The ultra-light and ultra-strong yet highly conductive materials are now known to us as graphene.

Indeed, most of the wreckage recovered in 1947 was comprised of materials that simply did not exist at that time, but are now relatively commonplace, such as Lexan-type polycarbonate sheets, carbon-fiber beams, ultra-light metallic micro-lattice nanomaterials, aluminized Mylar, graphene, and so on.

One somewhat mysterious aspect to the recovered material was its radiation signature, which did not match the expected terrestrial background radiation levels. It was not understood at the time that the energy signature observed was in fact consistent with a high-energy electrical discharge, which we now believe to have been the cause of the original explosion—and a primary reason why the materials closest to the blast were almost completely melted or burned.

Moreover, although not recognized at the time, recent discoveries about the physical design of the equipment and electronic components recovered from the scene are now seen to be consistent with equipment designed to monitor quantum electrodynamic field effects and diagnostic equipment designed to measure Lorentz forces generated by those high-energy fields.

Based on these findings, we must now entertain the possibility that these visitors—originally believed to be extra-terrestrial—may not have been space travelers at all, but have instead somehow come from either a different dimension or some future time.

If either of these possibilities is to be seriously considered, we must accept that the original crew were found to be most definitely of human origin—but with some unusual deviations from the standard human genome. Some of their physical characteristics, such as the lack of a belly button, are in fact suggestive of a distinctly different method of repro-duction and birth, while others, such as the blue skin of our female subject, suggest possible evolutionary adaptation to as-yet-unknown environmental variables. The subject has told us that this was the result of a virus, but fortunately this virus does not appear to be a danger at present.

"Thank goodness for that," said the presidential advisor.

"And," continued the major general, "although the visitor was conversant in the English language, she has never provided a satisfactory answer to explain how she got here or where she is from. In fact, the question of *why* she was unwilling to provide this information it itself still unanswered.

"What is *not* clear is why the visitors visited the Corona area in 1947. Our little blue guest never provided a satisfac-tory answer to that question, and our speculations based on the available evidence are at best inconclusive.

"The leading theories are:

- Concern about the nascent atomic age, which might explain the reported flyover of the Mountain Home Air Force Base near Nampa, Idaho.
- Environmental concerns, which might explain the apparent study of the snowpack on Mt. Rainier and the widely differing ecosystems of southern Idaho, north and southeastern Utah, and the plains of New Mexico.
- An interest in other emerging technologies, which might explain the flight path's close proximity to several strategic development centers, including Tacoma Washington, Groom Lake, Nevada, and the aforementioned AFB.

"However, I have a different theory that, while incomplete, is tantalizing in its prospects. I suggest that the June 24th UFO sighting over Mt Rainier, Washington, the July 4th sighting over Nampa, Idaho and the crash event that occurred later that night in Roswell, New Mexico are all related events. As evidence, I'd like to show you these locations on a map."

The slideshow advanced to an image of the western United States, with a diagonal line drawn, stretching from Washington state to New Mexico.

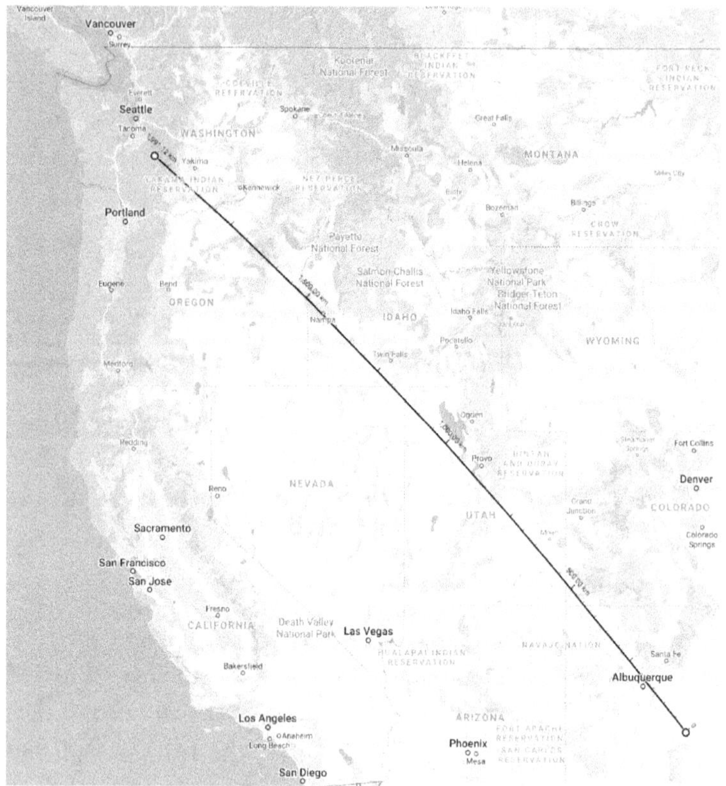

"On your upper left, that's Mount Rainier there—the location of the first reported sighting, at about 9200 feet, occurred just southwest of the peak, at 3:00 p.m. PST on June 24th. The path then proceeds southeast and passes through Nampa and the Mountain Home Air Force Base in Idaho, where the second sighting occurred, and one of our interceptors followed the radar image of a single craft—not a pack of nine, it should be noted—straight on down this way, where it ended up about 26 miles southeast of Corona, New Mexico. I believe that absolutely straight line is no coincidence.

"Our mathematical models based on calculation of the rotation and orbit of the earth, galaxial rotation and cosmic expansion support the theory that such a flight path would be a plausible outcome of efforts to geo-synchronize a time-shifted object by 17 sec.

"Put very simply, this would explain the extraordinarily high speed of the unidentified aerial phenomenon that was reported in Washington, Oregon and Idaho before it crashed just outside Roswell, New Mexico on that night in 1947.

"The 366 Wing scrambled a pair of interceptors and gave pursuit from the base at Mountain Home, however these pursuit vehicles were not able to maintain visibility of the fast-moving target for more than a minute or two, as the target was estimated to be moving roughly twice as fast as the interceptors. Fortunately, we had one on the ground at Holloman Air Force Base and managed to get that in the air in an expeditious fashion and were able keep eyes on the craft during the period before that, right up until the crash, which occurred right about *here*."

He tapped the area southeast of Corona on the map with his pointer.

* * *

July 1947

"God*dammit*. The war ends and practically every high-performance aircraft from here to Idaho is unavailable. The Las Vegas Army Airfield was officially deactivated in January, as was Woodring Field in Oklahoma. Clovis AAF is temporarily inactive. Fort Warren up in Wyoming halted their training program back in May. What else have we got?"

"What about Hill Field in Utah?"

"No, that's designated as long-term storage."

"Dammit. The AAF must have something capable of keeping up with these bogeys—they're practically underneath the projected flight path."

"That's not going to do it, sir; the target is clocking at more than 1000 miles per hour—our boys are topping out at about 600."

"What about the Skystreak[2]? I heard they just delivered one of those to Muroc Army Airfield."

"Great idea. And if that's not available, we'll just have to get the best we can. Tell 'em I need a P61 or better – *asap!*"

* * *

Did You Know?

Jim Ragsdale and his girlfriend Trudy Truelove gained local notoriety for their claim that they witnessed the crash first-hand and recovered pieces of the wreckage. Trudy was subsequently killed in an apparent truck accident and the materials from the wreckage she allegedly possessed are said to have disappeared around the time of her death.

Jim Ragsdale later testified in a sworn affidavit that his truck and his trailer were both stolen and all evidence of the wreckage he had recovered from the site was stolen after his house was broken into and ransacked by unknown parties.

---

[2] Douglas D-558-1 Skystreak

"My home was broken into, completely ransacked, and what was taken was the material, a gun and very little else of value."
—*Sworn Statement by Jim Ragsdale*

Col. DuBose (later promoted to General) has stated on the record that there was a cover-up and that the debris shown to the press was swapped.

I am convinced that the material recovered was some type of craft from outer space.
—*Affidavit of RAAF Information Officer Walter Haut*

Capt. Kimball of the 509th Division denied all knowledge of anything unusual occurring at the Roswell Army Air Field in the summer of 1947.

Frigg

2435

The accident at the Novelty Hill jumpstation deeply affected Karl Schraeder and the other workers at the lab. None of them had ever experienced an accidental death of even one co-worker—never mind *two*. While a nearly spotless 400-year safety record was something to be proud of, it especially embarrassed Karl that, as one of the "old guard" who had jumped forward many times, he had no one but himself to blame for the serious error that led to this terrible outcome.

Sure, mistakes happen, but he screwed up and lives were lost. It left him with an overwhelming sense of guilt as that cycle of failure played out time and time again in his mind. And the remote possibility that they might *not* be dead, but were instead marooned in 1947 was almost as bad. If that was the case, there was not a damned thing he could do about it. The fact that he got fired over this sad scenario seemed downright trivial by comparison.

Best-case scenario: If they were, by some miracle, still alive as a result of this terrible mistake, there would be absolutely no records showing proof of their citizenship. They'd be deported to god-knows-where or treated like illegal aliens, if not actual space aliens.

Far more likely, unfortunately, was the strong possibility that they were already dead. After all, people don't live for long when they're outdoors and completely unprotected against the elements in the Cascade Range of the Pacific Northwest in November. These two technicians weren't even wearing jackets out there. They probably died of hypothermia in less than 30 minutes.

That was the painful part of this whole episode. If the calculations were correct, they most likely dropped out of the sky near the radar station at Sunrise in the year 1947. The code that theoretically would vertically compensate for solid objects had never worked well, but it *might* have dropped them on the ground near Mount Rainier; there was just no way to be sure—it had never worked before.

If only a Bubblecraft had been available, he could have tried to send it back for a rescue attempt. Without it, there was just no way to get them back home to 2435 again. Even if he did somehow go back to find them, they would never be able to return home.

If he hadn't been fired, he might have been able to send a message to someone in charge there at the Sunrise radar station in 1947. But they couldn't do anything about it either, except probably cover up the whole incident, or at best, recover the bodies of two people for which there would be absolutely no records of any kind.

The fact that the facility—using technology that, for the most part, was nearly four hundred years old—was still in use was something of a technological miracle, anyway. Although it had been updated and upgraded with new safety features and conveniences along the way, the core field effect and communications technologies were still compatible with the field equations that Karl had worked on with Susan and the other members of the original team, nearly four centuries earlier.

That had been the biggest surprise: the chance discovery that the old army experiments in high-energy quantum fields back in 1947 had produced a field effect they could manipulate and communicate with. His eager pursuit of the possibilities inherent in that surprising discovery had directly led to this, his downfall.

Much had changed since then, of course. Although most of the original team had jumped forward several times, there had been those who, usually for reasons related to families or financial circumstances, had chosen to stay behind when others jumped away. So, there had been many funerals and belated graveyard visits, providing ample opportunity to reflect upon their changing places on the mortal coil.

The irony was that Karl himself had been instrumental in developing and implementing so many of the safety and procedural improvements to the jump tech since those early times, since the days when they could only jump in time-framesets that corresponded to specific values in the Fibonacci number set. There had been so many improvements since then!

Sometimes, the little things that weren't exactly mistakes had blown up into unanticipated problems. Back when Karl was working with the NASA engineers on the code that would eventually allow them to specify a jump gap of any arbitrary length of time, it seemed like a good idea to list the jump gap as a decimal-point value where a year equals 1.0 and thus months, weeks, days, and so on are decimal-point fractional values of that. He hadn't counted on other programmers not reading the commented code carefully and mistakenly thinking that 1.0 was the value for a day. It takes more than an 'Are you sure?' dialog box to work around that kind of mistake, as Marjorie Blint had discovered.

In fact, most of the improvements had been safety related. The old HELX accelerator had been serviced every 30 years or so, and, aside from needing a couple of sets of replacement magnets, a bunch of new capacitors, and a few switches and LEDs replaced now and then, was still working well.

Karl was used to his younger coworkers casting shade on 'this old relic.' In the eyes of the cerebrally augmented kids, the old machine was the technological equivalent of an antique steam engine.

"If you're going to insult this old beauty," Karl would tell them, "at least compare it to a trolley bus." Most of them had no idea what a trolley bus was, but Karl just told them to look it up. That got them off his back—for a while at least. And it was a more apt comparison.

The fact that the old beauty was still in operation in the 25th century was, in Karl's opinion, evidence that it had been a breakthrough in its time and undiminished as a remarkable achievement even after all this time. It had certainly provided him with steady and gainful employment. It had outlived his own children and their children's children, too. Thinking about those lives troubled him, though. Despite his occasional quarrels with George, Karl couldn't help but bear a certain grudging respect for the way George was able to change with the times. With George, it was always something new: some new augmentation technology, a new communications gadget, or a new girlfriend.

Karl had to admit to himself that, despite his own reticence regarding augmentation, it had clearly been good for George. Geo didn't seem to require the unplug-and-unwind down-time that many of his peers did. He just stayed plugged in all the time. And he didn't become an insufferable know-it-all or suffer from the manic panic like the others tended to, either.

Karl was pretty sure he wasn't built that way himself. His ex-wife had even cited this so-called manic behavior during her divorce proceedings, as she complained about what she called his "irritable mood, intense energy, racing thoughts, and other extreme and exaggerated behaviors."

He offered little defense to those points, other than to observe that they were also the traits of most of the other top-tier software engineers he knew, when an important project was on the line.

In contrast to the former Mrs. Schraeder, Li Yan had proven to be both tolerant of and sensitive to his moods. She wasn't especially romantic and, if he was being honest with himself, neither was he, but they got along well and there were benefits that went along with that.

Her absence during the period following the accident made the perceived impact of it that much greater. Li was off on yet another skill-set upgrade—this time, studying the vector field math she hoped would help crack the elusive problem of mapping a temporal jump point to a moving object. Beyond that lay the stretch goal of backwards time travel—maybe, someday.

Considering that the facility had been upgraded nearly a hundred times since it was founded in the twenty-thirties, the operational safety record of the Novelty Hill facility was outstanding. Aside from a few minor workplace injuries, workers at the lab had enjoyed a remarkably safe workplace environment and a clean jump-safety record ever since the deck-clearing signaling protocols had been automated nearly 50 years earlier. So, not a bad run.

The worst problems during that period had, in fact, been security related. It had become extremely common for bad actors to poison search results to allow verification of false identities and fake cover stories. Criminal activity was particularly prevalent on the Russian and Chinese jumpstations, with the latter reported as seeing a 340 percent increase in cases of false identity or illicit activity in the two-year period following its initial launch. Attempted transfers of illegal weapons were reportedly up more than 600 percent. And given the strong likelihood of corruption, cronyism, and other payoffs in those state-sponsored enterprises, those estimates were probably far from accurate.

Such shenanigans were an issue at Andna's own jumpstations, too. There were huge discrepancies between the number of jumps recorded and the number of $180,000 jump fees collected. So, either some parties inside the organization were pocketing a great deal of that money, or there were a lot of off-the-record jumps being made.

It was a persistent annoyance to Karl that this marked the second time he had been fired, and he feared this one might not be so easy to come back from. Last time, he had been made an example of for helping George make a single unpaid jump at the old Princeton facility, when the two of them were the ones primarily responsible for keeping the damned thing running anyway. He'd been caught by a security bot, which recorded his ID when it was used to run a post-jump diagnostic. He'd been found guilty of a breach of protocol and fired via email by the AI arbiter without even a chance to explain. If the intent of that was to dissuade others from trying something similar, the gesture had certainly been in vain. All it did was teach everyone to delete the logs after every test.

Fortunately, the technical director at the Novelty Hill facility had been willing to overlook what he called a minor breach of protocol. He was much more interested in Karl's unique insights into the HELX codebase, with its hundreds of patches and updates. Karl was able to make a convincing argument that he and Li Yan were both essential to the project, as evidence that ongoing funding was required and worthwhile. That was true, but even so, the last few ten-year funding cycles had seen their share of cutbacks and constraints. The fact that the new management team from EON Research was once again setting up a "formal education program" to get around government restrictions on unpaid interns was ample proof of that.

* * *

Watching what Karl was going through, Li Yan became something of a mental health advocate and activist for jumpers. As an only child whose parents had lived and died in China, she was somewhat less invested in family relations than Karl, George, Susan, Amir, or any of the other jumpers she knew. But she'd seen a pattern emerge among those who had jumped forward far enough to outlive their siblings or children. The result was often depression, anxiety, doubt and sometimes even dysphoria. As an engineer, she had no pretensions about being an expert in psychology, but to her layperson's eye, it seemed similar to imposter syndrome: 'I don't have the updated skills I need to be competitive; I'm not competent enough to deserve this job; I don't deserve to outlive my children/siblings, I doubt my own worthiness,' and so on.

And in many cases, those who jumped forward more than a few years *did* lack the modern skills that they needed to get a decent job. The farther forward they jumped, the worse the problem got, and by the beginning of the 25th century, only those who were cerebrally augmented got the good jobs, anyway.

Karl had come to Li Yan at one such juncture, expressing his worries that he was an outmoded relic. He said he was 'not very interested in keeping up with the kids who have to get wired up to the big mac just to get a damn job.'

Li Yan took a pragmatic approach: she took skills training after every jump to ensure that she was up to date on the technical side, and she always made sure to secure a future role before jumping. Plans change, of course, so there had been a few glitches during that 400-year period, but overall, she felt fortunate that she still had a job, and was still young enough to enjoy the new worlds she jumped into. Well, to a point.

When you jump from one culture straight into another one, the differences seem all the more glaringly obvious.

Li had jumped forward at more or less the same pace as Karl. It was far more fun to have someone to share the new experiences with. But when Karl ended up with the Genetech virus and turned blue, she could immediately see a difference in the way people treated him—like a pariah. The same was true when she started showing up at higher education classes where she was the only one who wasn't cerebrally augmented. Suddenly, she was the one getting the second-class citizen treatment from the Augs.

At least George didn't treat her like that. But then again, she tried to see as little of George as possible.

* * *

"Come with me, please. *Please*," begged Karl.

"No! Absolutely not. I haven't even finished my last course. I won't go. It's not fair and you know it. Why don't you just stay? I've still got a job; you'll find something else. Maybe you can work remotely, like George does."

"I can't. Li, please come with me. I need you."

"Oh please. You say that *now*. That is not fair. I'm busy.

Anyway, just slow down for a moment. What is the point? What is jumping again actually going to solve?"

"I have to do something about Frigg and Leonid. I've just got to."

"What can you possibly do?"

"I'm going to find George. He must know how to solve this problem. I've got to find George."

"Well, you don't need to jump around to do that. He's got agents all over the place."

* * *

11 |

Reconnaissance

"The theory of quantum mechanics forces us [...] to drop the assumption of the absolute character of knowledge about nature, and to deal with the principle of causality independently of this assumption.

Quantum mechanics has therefore not contradicted the law of causality at all, but has clarified it and has removed from it other principles which are not necessarily connected to it."

— GRETE HERMANN, THE FOUNDATIONS OF QUANTUM
MECHANICS IN THE PHILOSOPHY OF NATURE

"When a candidate matches a target profile with a 40 percent or higher confidence rating, you are to open a case number and engage the candidate and attempt to verify details matching those of target. Gain their confidence and report all activities, including those involving or requested of third parties."

The man behind the desk watched as Surya opened her notebook and clicked her pen. "It's very important that you follow the guidance in the training about not leaving any hard evidence of your covert activities. None whatsoever. That means don't create written notes or expose anything else that could leave any sort of a trail. No internet histories, no phone call logs, no emails—not even anonymized ones. Single-use burner phones only. If you receive correspondence from HQ, burn it after reading. Leave no evidence, understood?"

Surya nodded.

"Any questions?"

Surya put the pen away, feeling more than a little embarrassed. All this stuff had been covered in the training videos. She just didn't realize that these rules of engagement applied here. "Could you maybe clarify the recommended sequence of hinted suggestions used during target identification?"

"Certainly. As may recall from the training, you'll want to be very subtle when attempting to convey an idea indirectly. You might, for example, imply that you'll free during a period when you believe the target is planning a trip or a pickup or drop-off of some sort. Even if they don't invite you along on the trip, chances are good that you may learn that they have plans, or where they are headed.

"Conversely, supposing we provide you with intel in the form of, say, search data that indicates the target might be looking for travel arrangements or accommodations, you could reach out and subtly insinuate that you're headed in that general direction and might be open to bringing him or her along. That sort of thing.

"We recommend starting with opportunities that are hard to refuse, but sound very plausible. In the case of Mr. Gunderson, for example, you might simply intimate that you'll be in the area. Chances are good he'll want to see you. Any suggestion that lets you communicate with the target on a topic that's near and dear to their heart both before and *after* a planned meeting has occurred is a best-case scenario."

"So," she asked, "supposing I know that Gunderson is planning a trip to Seahaven, should I say I'm on a boat that's heading up to Newfoundland, or just let him know that I'm open to the idea of him catching a ride with me the next time I'm heading up that way?"

"No, it's better to just mention the boat very casually, as if it's this new job, where you go all over. Let him think the idea of catching a ride with you is his idea. You know, if a target feels comfortable, it's easier than it sounds."

He paused and studied her facial expression for a second. "All you really want to do is find out exactly when and where he'll be, and if possible, who he's meeting with."

"I understand," she said.

"You'll alternate between being stationed at one of the North American jump stations as a greeter and following up with target candidates."

He lifted the top page of paper on his clipboard and looked at the details on the page underneath it it. "You'll be starting off at the, ah, original Andna site in Princeton, New Jersey. There's no commercial traffic going through there, so your candidates will be—or at least should be—employees or contractors.

"You'll be looking for any suspicious activities that might indicate the theft, sale, or other compromise of military property or any other proprietary information.

"We think that there may be one or more parties on the original engineering team that worked there who are or were violating their non-disclosure agreements, and may also be selling or distributing trade secrets and military IP."

"IP?"

"Sorry—intellectual property."

"Ah, yes, of course. Thanks."

"We think it's one of the parties with Global Admin status at that lab. There are, we believe, only four individuals with that level of administrative access: Karl Schraeder, George Gunderson, Li Yan Zhang and Erich Rössler. We don't really think Rössler is a target, but you never know. So, keep your eyes open."

"Will do."

* * *

When George heard that Andna LLC had purchased the Hexamer, a defunct oil drilling platform—technically, a concrete deep-water gravity-based structure—off the east coast of Newfoundland, he was curious. What would AndnaCorp want with an oil drilling operation—and a defunct one at that?

Annoyingly, the government office responsible for the original registration of the Hexamer was not compliant with the standard protocol his agents used to communicate with third-party registrars. Worse, the office was not contactable via any form of automated electronic interaction protocol the agents tried. For all his high-tech communication capabilities, George was forced to reach out manually via the contact number information in the government records and eventually got a response back—by old-fashioned snail mail, of all things.

The agents were, however, able to retrieve a few related news stories that helped provide a little background information about the sale. A story in a publication called *Maven* said that Nolan Stern, having inherited half of the assets of Andna LLC, had purchased the Hexamer—which, before being shut down, had been the world's largest deep-sea gravity-based structure and the record holder for the largest and most complex engineering project in history—and established Seahaven as the smallest independent nation-state in the world. It was the largest *and* the smallest.

What an ideal place to build a jump station, thought George. And, by the sound of it, Nolan Stern might just have the money to make it happen. George had his agents look up 'friends with a boat.' It wasn't long before Surya, an occasional girlfriend, responded. She was headed that way in April and sure, she could take him there.

* * *

12

Seahaven

2431

Seabirds wheeled over the cliffs of North Head on the east coast of Newfoundland, winging their way south across the Narrows toward Cahill Point. They gracefully turned past the majestic shoreline, passing low over the water in the early morning light. Surya Byrne, the 2nd Mate of the RV Solair, studied the birds through her binoculars as the SWATH[3] research vessel sliced through the waves on its way east of St. Johns Bay.

She pointed out a pair of dark gulls to George as the birds passed the boat. "See those birds?" she asked him, her voice rising over the sound of the electric motors and crashing waves. "Those used to be known as Leach's Storm-Petrels," she said.

"What are they called now?" asked George.

---

[3] Small Waterplane Area Twin Hull

She shrugged. "That was an old colonial name. We just call them Storm Petrels now. There used to be millions of them on the islands along the coast in these parts and, although the numbers have declined significantly in the past couple of hundred years due to the weather, they are still the most common bird around here. You get used to seeing them. The dark color makes them pretty easy to identify. And they almost never follow boats, which is a bit unusual."

She scanned the horizon ahead. "Ah, there it is."

196 miles offshore—in international waters far outside the 12-mile territorial limit—loomed the giant multi-level

hexagonal deck of what was once an oil drilling platform known as the Hexamer.

"Just wait here. This won't take long."

The captain's voice crackled over the speaker. "Out fenders, starboard side."

"Aye aye." Surya pushed the bumpers over the side of the right pontoon of the twin-hulled craft.

"Prepare the lines.

"Ready."

"Prepare to haul in."

Moments later, the crew had the boat tied up securely to the mooring rings on the sea platform and Surya crossed the gangway carrying her seabag and a bag of trash. "Welcome back, Surya," called a blue-skinned woman standing on the dockside ramp. "Nice to see you again. How are the new batteries doing on the Solair?"

"Really good," said Surya. "It's a big improvement. We really appreciated your help with that."

She turned to George. "I'll catch up with you as soon as I finish up here," she said. "You go on ahead."

"This is my friend George Gunderson," Surya said to the woman as George disembarked. "This is his first time here."

"Ah, marvelous! Welcome to Seahaven, Mister Gunderson. My name is Miran Wen. Are you from Newfoundland?"

"No," said George. "I'm from New Jersey, actually."

"Well, we're pleased to have you here. We don't get too many visitors out this way at this time of year. Most of our contact is electronic during the stormy season between November and March. How was the weather coming in?"

"It was a little rough, but this boat handled it really well."

"Did you run into that rainstorm on the way here?"

"Yeah, the skies were pretty dark for a while."

"I see you've come in on the Solair. Are you part of the research team?"

"No, not directly. I'm an engineer, myself. I used to work with Surya, and, uh, she offered me a ride out here."

"Allow me to tell you little about our home here on the sea. Seahaven was established as a principality in 2429 and we now exist as the world's smallest legal sovereign state. We have our own postage stamps, currency, and passports—all of which are digital—and we bestow honors and titles of nobility as the prince sees fit."

"Ah yes, the prince. And what is his name?"

"Prince Nolan of the House of Stern."

"Ah. I knew his parents. His father and I worked together, in fact."

"That is most interesting. So, you must know his sister, Ceryl?"

"Yes, I do. Do you know if Ceryl is still in contact with a woman by the name of Susan Everett?"

"Oh, Susan the storyteller? Oh yes, we all like her stories very much. I will ask the prince if he knows when she is expected to visit again and if it is soon, I will be sure to let you know. Do you know how long you are planning to stay at Seahaven?"

"Well, that all depends. I have a business proposal I would like to present to the government here. Do you know who I might talk to about business affairs and that sort of thing?"

"One moment," said Miran. "I will find someone who can help you with that."

"It's not urgent. This is something of a holiday for me. I'm just pleased to hear that you know some of my old friends."

"I'm delighted to hear that. I'll be sure to pass along the contact information you will require to make an appointment. Is there anything I can tell you about the lodging and dining offerings available here?"

"No, that's fine. I already have a room booked at the Seaview Lodge. I believe there's a cafeteria of some sort on the premises."

"There is—and the fish and chips are very good. An old family recipe. Or if you prefer, there's a complete selection of vegan offerings—all grown onboard. I'm sure you'll be pleased.

"Enjoy your stay, Mister Gunderson. You'll follow that yellow line up those stairs and it will take you up to the top level, past the recreation area right to the visitors center. The Seaview Lodge is just on the other side of that. I'll arrange for someone to contact you there, once you've checked in."

Behind her towered a truly massive staircase, climbing a hundred steps per level, with nine levels in all. George climbed up the stairs past the first few levels, which were dominated by the massive concrete and steel pylons supporting the structure. Then, above that, he passed by three levels seemingly consisting of nothing but huge boilers, pumps and pipes. Then three more levels revealing more staircases, some lights, and more pipes. There were pipes everywhere. On the second level were what looked like generators and HVAC equipment.

And, finally, on the top level, a large building dominated the southern end of the platform. It was rather crudely painted with white letters that must have been at least 12 feet high, spelling out the word SEAHAVEN in large squared-off block letters. Just beyond it, a vast crane rose above the surface of the deck and, near it, a trio of truck-sized forklifts moved pallets from shipping containers. He estimated the entire platform, including the massive pylons and gravity base that extended 80 meters down to the sea floor below it, must have been more than 225 meters high, not counting the container handling gantry crane (adding another 40 meters or so!) or the five-storey building on the top deck. Massive.

George followed the yellow painted line past the main building to a somewhat more modern-looking structure labeled REC CENTRE. He peered for a moment through the window, trying to ascertain what inside. He could see a few exercise bikes and treadmills, but no one was using the equipment.

Finally, he reached a sign on the huge platform that said VISITORS CENTRE. It, too, appeared to be deserted. It did, however, have a helpful map painted on the outside wall. And just as Miriam had said, the Seaview Lodge was straight ahead.

* * *

The lodge, at least, had a person at the desk. Two young women, in fact. One was talking on a telephone; the other greeted George with a friendly smile.

"Good morning! Are you checking in?"

"Yes. Reservation for George Gomez."

"I have that right here. Three nights, deluxe sea view room, west side, one double bed. Does that sound all right?"

"Yes, thank you."

"Do you have any luggage?"

"Just this," he said, waving his sports bag.

"Would you like us to take that to your room for you?"

"No, I've got it, thanks."

"We've got your credit information here; everything looks to be in good order. Checkout time is 11 a.m. on Thursday. Is there anything else I can help you with?"

"No, thank you."

"Enjoy your stay."

* * *

The room was humble but reasonably clean and, although the bed and décor weren't exactly up to the usual standards befitting a 'deluxe' room, they were certainly serviceable enough for his needs.

The place was reasonably quiet, too. George occasionally heard a mechanical clunk or scraping noise, presumably from the nearby shipping containers, but it wasn't bad. He couldn't hear any splashing sounds coming from sea level, hundreds of meters below.

The in-room entertainment options were far from state of the art. There was an old flat-screen TV and a small stack of books on the nightstand. He picked up one labeled *Visitors Guide*.

It was a three-ring binder containing a rundown of the

various services available to Seahaven guests: Internet, telephone and print services, child care, laundry, yoga, exercise, and prayer services. They seemed to be big on prayer services here—there were services offered every day of the week, and twice on Sundays.

A page listing room service and dining options reminded George that he hadn't eaten since they left the mainland. He messaged Surya to find out what she was up to.

I'm at the diner, she replied.

On my way, he wrote.

The entrance to the diner was down a short flight of stairs from the main floor of the lodge. Surya waved to George from a booth near the window; he smiled and slid into the seat opposite her.

She had changed clothes; her blonde hair had that look it got when it was freshly showered.

"How's the salad?" he asked.

"It's very good. Really fresh. Try one of these cherry tomatoes—they're awesome."

"Mm, that is good. I haven't eaten all day."

"Me neither," she said between mouthfuls. "Don't mind me."

He browsed through the menu. "It all looks good. I think I'll go with the all-day breakfast."

"There's a waitress around here somewhere. She'll come around. With a coffee pot, hopefully."

After George finished eating and Surya had finally had her fill of coffee, they got to talking about how they each came to know the self-styled prince.

George explained that he had known Prince Nolan's grandfather. "I worked for him for several years back in Princeton," he said.

"The Sterns have some property there, near the university, don't they?"

"Yes. I've been there. I know Andrew Stern pretty well."

"Andrew—that's Nolan's father, right?"

"Yep. I've met Nolan's sister Ceryl and their mother Kaedra, too."

"Wow. You're in tight with these guys, aren't you?"

"Well, like I said, we go back a long way."

He didn't bother mention exactly how long, as he doubted she would have believed him.

Prince Nolan's grand plan had always been to keep the dollars rolling in, so it wasn't hard for George to arrange a business meeting with the Seahaven Business Development Council. The prince didn't attend these meetings, but he often listened in surreptitiously. When George got back to his hotel room later that evening, a notification was waiting for him that his request for a meeting with the council had been approved for 9 o'clock a.m. the following morning. He sent confirmation that he would attend and sent a 'meeting with prince confirmed' message to Surya.

At the meeting the next morning, George was being a little bit difficult. He wasn't sure whether Prince Nolan was aware of his father's use of the temporal displacement tech and he wasn't willing to discuss specifics with anyone else—certainly not a haggle-bot. He insisted that the prince be present during the meeting.

The Business Development Council, on the other hand, weren't willing to assure him that the prince would attend the meeting. In fact, they assured him that he *never* listened to 'cold call' pitches without them first being vetted by the council.

Fortunately, the Business Development Council didn't appear prejudicial of George's request that they sign a non-disclosure agreement before learning the details of the proposal.

When the prince heard George's claim that he was the original developer of the Bubblecraft/Jumpgate technology, the legendary exploits of his father began to make sense. 400 years old and seemingly immortal. Fighter of monsters. Prophet of the ages. It all made sense. With this tech, he, too, could build such a legend.

He signaled his representatives that he wanted them to strike a deal. And so, after George made it clear that he had the goods and the credentials to back up his claims, they made a deal for the rapid development of what George claimed would be the world's first commercial jumpgate.

Predictably, Surya was eager to learn what went down at George's meeting with the prince.

George had no intention of telling her the whole truth. You have to play these things close to your chest. He kept things vague, and confirmed only that a deal had been made to handle commercial goods. That much was true and that was enough.

* * *

Later that evening, Surya was alone in her room, speaking on the telephone. "The deal was made. I will. Goodbye."

* * *

After the deal with the prince was sealed, George extended his three-night stay at Seahaven indefinitely and spent the time arranging for the parts and components he required to complete the project. His reengineered design was based in part on the second-generation Bubblecraft/Starjumper tech, so it didn't require as much physical space as the original HELX accelerator's 'toroidal ring' design; its power requirements were lower, as well. Both of these attributes, as well as the innate modularity of the Bubblecraft field generator, made it well-suited for deployment onboard a deep-sea platform.

The Solair research vessel he'd arrived on with Surya had commitments elsewhere, so he and Surya had one last dinner-date and shared a bed together that third night. By the time George woke up, Surya was already onboard the Solair, headed westward again. She'd left a folded piece of paper on the bed stand, though. A pucker in pale pink lipstick signed a note that said 'Till we meet again....'

The delivery, assembly, and testing of the components took five months; training the maintenance and operations staff took another two months. Finally, in the late autumn of 2431, the system was ready for operation.

The prince had commissioned studies of all the ways that the 'jump forward' tech could be used to add value to the platform. The list presented to him extolled the virtues of everything from "life extension" medical procedures to Seahaven health club memberships and "fountain of youth" vacations. "Imagine," George said, "A luxury vacation spot where guests can go for any length of time, and come back scarcely looking a day older."

* * *

13

Solar Storm

Four years later...

News journalist and social media influencer Mayleen Li and her cameraman stood on the top deck of Seahaven. She held the microphone in her chilly hand and read from the portable teleprompter.

"The storm of the century is brewing and the *fin de siècle* survivalist fanatics are convinced this is The Big One. What began as a converted drilling platform once known as the Hexamer has now been fashioned by force of will into a business venture worth untold millions of dollars that would be illegal were it not operated in international waters, far outside the purview of American rules of law.

"From its beginning as the deep-sea home of what some have called a radical survivalist cult to a multibillion-dollar haven for pornography and internet gambling, the stunning success story that is Seahaven is one of fueled by the promises of their charismatic leader, Nolan Stern, a self-styled prince born to the son of wealthy American industrialist Isaac Stern.

"Prince Nolan is the kingpin of this porn and gambling app empire operating since 2429 outside legal jurisdictions in international waters off the southeast coast of Newfoundland.

"Convinced that the world is hell-bent on the road to ruin, Stern has amassed a team of renegade researchers, scientists, artists and technicians—radical activists who say they are amassing the largest treasure trove of genetic information ever assembled from around the world."

"Cut. Let me try that bit again."

"Ready? Action."

"The Seahaven platform is the self-styled prince's own little autocracy, and he their benevolent dictator. The prince is said to be obsessed with youth and is rumored to have spent a considerable portion of his wealth on anti-ageing research. In fact, Stern refuses to discuss his real age, but is believed to be in his mid-forties. And, you have to admit: he's looking good for his age.

"Another area the enigmatic leader of this isolated community refuses to discuss is the life he left behind before buying the Hexamer and founding Seahaven. Although W6 has not been able to track down the identity of Stern's former wife, rumors persist that the policy of polygamy that has made Annatarian politics so controversial in this country is an edict straight from the top. For W6 News, I'm Mayleen Li."

"And cut."

After recording and submitting the segment, Mayleen and her cameraman retreated to an area protected from the cold

Atlantic winds to discuss the next shot. Her phone rang. It was the producer.

"What do you mean you can't use it?"

"Come on, Ed. People love a little controversy. Besides, he's not an advertiser, he's a nut. All right, I'll grant you that. He could be. But... Yes, I know he's rich and influential." She listened for a moment and sighed. "All right. I'll call when I've got it." She hung up. "Argh. I'll rewrite it again."

* * *

Outside, her cameraman waited. "I'll try and get you in there later today," she told him. "Until I talk to the Media Manager, there's not much I can do right now. I'm going back in there." She looked at her watch. "Find Jack and tell him I'll meet you both at the copter in half an hour, okay?" Maybe get a few more shots of the rougher looking areas, okay?"

He nodded and, lifting the camera onto his shoulder, turned to leave.

* * *

George had flown in by helicopter several times over the past couple of years but he had come in on the supply boat this time and was surprised to see someone other than Miran on dock duty. This young woman gave him the whole 'welcome to Seahaven' speech and courtesy treatment, apparently unaware that he'd been a fairly regular guest and contractor at the platform for the past four years. It had changed a lot during this time, with the building of the new hotel and casino. Over the past year, in particular, the latest round of upgrades had been impressive indeed. And of course, the world's first commercial jump station was nearly ready to begin service for paying customers.

"Well, enjoy your stay, Mister Gunderson. Just take the elevator up to level 3 and it will take you right to the main floor of the casino. The Seaview Grand is just on the other side of that. I'll arrange for someone to contact you there, once you've checked in."

A glimmering capsule of glass and metal descended and the elevator doors opened, revealing a luxurious wood and brass interior below an expansive panel of wraparound glass. The elevator door slid shut and it smoothly ascended, passing by the maintenance and engineering decks and gliding to a stop outside an area labeled as Seahaven Control—a control center on the top deck at the southern end of the platform. Just beyond it, where a large stack of shipping containers had dominated the deck the last time George had been here, was now a vast apron marked with a huge white 'H'—it was now a proper landing area for helicopters. Everything looked newly painted.

When George got to the casino, he walked past a windowed room he hadn't seen before. It was filled with vast racks of computers. He wondered if they were there for show, or whether these glass walls were really secure enough for such an operation. He peered for a moment through the window into the control room, trying to ascertain what types of computers and operating systems were in use. He could see people working at the other end of the long glass-walled room, surrounded by flat screens, but they were too far away to notice a knock on the glass, if he had even dared to be so bold. It was clear, however, that many of the screens were displaying what appeared to be online gambling operations and pornography website applications; others seemed to be server monitoring software packages.

On the other side of the casino, the hotel and restaurant offerings had also been substantially upgraded since the last time George had been here.

"Is there anything I can tell you about the hotel and restaurant offerings available here?"

"Thank you. I already have a room booked at the Seaview Grand. There's a new restaurant of some sort on the premises, isn't there?"

"There is—and it's very good. World-class seafood, fresh caught every day, prepared by our executive chef to the highest culinary standards. I'm sure you'll be pleased."

* * *

Miran was in the control center, eyeing the Doppler radar scope. The meteorologist typed in coordinates on a keyboard and frowned as he examined the satellite data displayed on an adjacent screen.

The meteorologist studied the on-screen data and addressed his colleague at the radio console. "This is definitely bad."

His colleague rolled his wheeled chair closer to the monitor for a better look. "Miran," he said, "you'd better tell Prince Nolan. He needs to know."

"I don't think we should bother him with this yet."

"No, I promised him I would tell him if any emergency messages came in. We're picking up warnings from all over. Even the BBC is broadcasting on the emergency band now."

He cupped his hand over the headset and listened intently

to the shortwave radio signal. "Terrible reception," he declared. He tried a couple of different settings to no avail.

The meteorologist pointed to a spike in the new data coming in on the screen. "Look at the radio flux progression over the last 15 minutes," he said. "It looks like an M-class or maybe even an X-class solar flare. Whatever it is, there's a serious geomagnetic storm brewing. Solar winds are way up, and X-rays are, too. The reception difficulties are most likely going to get a lot worse—and if it's an X-class event, it could knock out the satellites and the network entirely. I'm going to send out a general alert to the hotels and the casino."

"Have you seen anything this big before?" Miran asked the radio operator.

"Yeah, I've been through a few fairly big coronal mass ejection events. You know, ones that caused radio blackouts and other types of RF interference. They weren't satellite killers, though. But I remember reading about the really big one that happened back in April 1999. We studied it in school. The energy from that one was something like ten million times greater than the energy released from a volcanic explosion."

"I strongly doubt that this one is as powerful as that."

"I hope you're right about that."

"In any case, I'm calling it in." He picked up a hotline phone.

"You are blessed. Prince Nolan's office."

"Hi Chaissie. This is Matt in the meteorological office. Patch me through to Prince Nolan, please."

"Will do."

* * *

In his opulent office, surrounded by quasi-religious arti-facts, the prince picked up the phone. "You are blessed. Speak to me." He was a tanned and physically fit man, dressed in his usual weekday attire: loose-fitting Egyptian cotton cloth-ing with a long gold and black embroidered vest that looked vaguely Middle Eastern in style and two gold rings on each of his hands.

"Your highness, it's Matt in the meteorological office. As you may know, sir, we are due for some heavy weather. How-ever, there's a complication: there is a major solar weather event that is interfering with our communications and net-work services. Yes sir, quite serious. We've put out a general advisory to the hotels and casino regarding expected service interruptions or outages. Yes sir, we will. On the hour, until the situation normalizes. Thank you, sir, same to you. Goodbye."

Whatever it was, the solar storm was creating a wide range of solar-terrestrial effects, including disturbances that knocked out satellites, power spikes and power plant shutdowns, and severe disruptions in radio and television transmissions and, most notably, weather disturbances all over the bright side of the earth. Meteorologists predicted massive storms all over.

As well as all these extraordinary solar events were other unusual electromagnetic disturbances in the ionosphere and earth's magnetic fields. Matt warned that it was shaping up to be one of the most serious solar weather events of the century. He cautioned the prince that degradation or possibly even complete loss of internet connectivity looked increasingly likely.

Prince Nolan listened intently. As he held the phone, he twirled an old-fashioned globe on his desk.

"Don't worry." He pressed the hook of the phone, then snapped into action, punching the receptionist button.

"Chaissie, get me Stevie."

Three decks below, in the heart of the compound, a room full of devotees sat cross-legged in meditation. Only one, an oriental woman, was dressed in business attire. She opened her eyes and watched the others as an outsider would. The others, with eyes closed, were dressed in purple and gold cloaks.

The group leader paused her guided prayer, her silent pager vibrating on her hip. "Peace be with you" she said as she stood up and quietly exited the room.

The Asian woman, her eyes open, watched the instructor's exit intently. *Something* was up, and it looked important. She got up and followed the instructor out the door, slipping on her shoes as she left. She stayed far enough behind her to be inconspicuous and followed the woman to a hallway labeled Antechamber. The instructor opened a door there and entered the room and quietly closed the door.

Mayleen Li, the well-known social media influencer and journalist, had been invited onboard the platform as part of what had become for the Havenites a yearly pre-season ritual: a dog and pony show for the media, designed to generate articles in all the most influential channels. This week it was 'luxury lifestyle' journalists who were aboard; in the weeks ahead, it would be video crews, podcasters, and vloggers.

The luxury lifestyle segment was one of the only areas of the magazine market that still published paper, but even so, the market wasn't what it used to be. Mayleen now had to freelance, writing for both the top-tier mags and the wanna-bes like *Maven* and *#TheGoodLife*. But they paid for her travel, food and hotel, so it wasn't all bad. Writing about travelling the world, staying in the finest hotels and eating at the best restaurants was hard work, but it had its perks. Some of the gigs were better than others, of course. The luxury automobile market was a total sausage fest—and you had to give the cars back when you were done testing. Same with the yachts and the jets. Even the high-end jewelry market was tough to catch a break in these days. They just weren't gifting like they used to. Give me the gigs covering high-end spas, hotels and restaurants any day, she thought.

Still, it got lonely sometimes on these junkets. There were a lot of creeps in the upper echelons. So, it was George's good fortune that Mayleen was looking for someone to talk to that evening at the bar.

They compared their favorite luxury destinations; she lamented the haters that were an inevitable part of her world. George was a good listener and fed her a constant stream of the glib attitude and unwavering attention her media-saturated ego required. He asked her what she knew about Prince Nolan Stern and hit the jackpot.

As it turned out, she was writing a major piece on the prince, and had been researching his affairs for months. The trouble was, she couldn't use most of the good stuff.

She explained to George the ridiculous restrictions placed

upon her. The publisher she was working with on the Seahaven story frowned upon disclosure of any information—on any topic whatsoever!—that could be perceived as critical of a featured client, product or service. Blindsiding the client was simply not done. These days, you couldn't afford to be too critical of an advertiser. You'd just end up blacklisted and barred from future events. She had been given utterly unambiguous instructions that, for this gig, she had to adhere to the strict boundaries of conduct specified in the *Seahaven Media Guidelines*. Or else.

One of the guidelines was that the prince was not to be asked about his parents any other member of his immediate family.

Another was that the prince was not to be asked about age or any other questions regarding his corporeal form. Speculation about whether he was or wasn't aug'ed was strictly forbidden. The prince, it seemed, wanted to be seen as the monarchal ideal of both groups.

Only his closest associates and advisors, such as Chaissie and Miran, knew the truth: he was in fact cerebrally augmented and this was the reason for his estrangement from his parents (and yet, ironically, for his success, as well). His mother, in particular, saw it as her own failing that her son had turned his back on the Annatarian Way.

In his role as leader of the Havenites and founder of Annatarianism, Nolan's father had largely been absent during the childhoods of Nolan and his sister Ceryl.

They had studied the precepts of Annatarian philosophy as their father wished, and Ceryl had become a source of pride to him as she followed her mother Kaedra in the gentle art of storytelling.

Nolan, however, was fascinated by the modern world, and spent much of his boyhood consorting with Volvists. When he dared to marry one and they gave birth to the blue-fleshed monster child Frigg, that was too much. He, and Miran Wen, who was the child's birthfree mother, were banished from the House of Wen forever.

Birthfree motherhood was a Volvist practice frowned upon by Havenites. Children thus conceived were grown like clones, but with genetic contributions from at least two parents. You could always spot a birthfree child by its lack of a belly button.

Earlier that day, Mayleen had pulled no punches during her final interview with the prince. "Some of your former supporters have spoken out in opposition of your beliefs and your tactics," she said. "You have been called a cult; accused of mistreating and misleading your followers. How do you respond to these accusations?"

Miran had been called into doing duty as chief of damage control when the media handlers heard the kinds of questions Mayleen was asking.

"The platform," Miran explained, "has its own laws and derives a significant portion of its operating income from its proprietary offerings, including internet gambling operations and other 'edge of the law' activities." When pressed to explain what 'edge of the law' meant exactly, she said, "that is to say, entirely lawful in our geographic location." Fine words from the operator of a highly internet-centric gambling concern.

When asked about Prince Nolan's inner circle, she named former Nobel prize-winning geneticist and Seahaven's Chief Scientist Errol Cummings, Training coordinator Stevie Lyle and Chaissie Morrow, his personal assistant.

Mayleen characterized her as "the woman who may know him best, his longtime companion and personal assistant, Ms. Chaissie Morrow."

"Let's wrap it up," shouted the cameraman. "Ready?"

As Miran fretted and Mayleen straightened her windblown hair in front of the Visitor's Center sign, her cameraman gave the countdown. "Rolling in 3... 2...."

Mayleen continued where she had left off. "Around them," she said, "hundreds of others volunteer their time and donate huge sums to further a utopian dream of the world according to Nolan Stern."

"Got it, good. Let's get out of here!" yelled the cameraman as he unplugged the external microphone and got the camera back into its bag. Mayleen watched a group of frantic people run across the deck in front of her. That would have made a great shot, she thought.

* * *

14

2435: Homecoming

"We have to leave—*now!*" shouted Jack, barely audible over the whistling wind. "It's getting too dangerous to stay. We take off in three minutes."

Mayleen looked at her watch. "Can you come back after the storm passes?"

"Sure, I guess. It might take a few days."

"I'm going to stay, then. I'll be all right."

"If you say so. But Dave's coming with me, right?" Jack turned to the cameraman and held up three fingers. "Three minutes, Dave!"

Mayleen shook her head. "I need you here, Dave!" she yelled, holding her arms wide, awe-struck at the spectacle unfolding around her, as deck chairs and roof panels lifted off and flew away like birds into the mist. "I need you to shoot this absolute, utter mayhem—it's crazy!"

"Yes, it is—but not in a good way. It's not safe. We should leave—immediately!"

"But Dave, I...." A huge gust of wind and a massive wave knocked her over before she could finish the sentence and swept her off the ship into the squall. The helicopter slid perilously closer to the edge.

"Oh my god," moaned Dave, lowering the camera. He could hardly believe the scene he'd just recorded.

Jack grimaced and started up the copter's engine. "We've got to take off—now!"

Dave climbed aboard, hoisting the camera to his shoulder again for another shot as the blades spun up to speed. Before him, a panorama of mayhem was playing out. The helicopter attempted to take off but another huge gust of wind tipped it over. The helicopter's airframe buckled and the rotor blades smashed, useless. Jack crawled out of the smoking wreckage and, struggling against the gale-force winds, attempted to pull the cameraman free. He managed to lift the broken airframe and pull the wounded man away from the twisted fuselage. "Get the camera," Dave pleaded.

As the apocalyptic storm built in power, Nolan and Miran were down on the second level, stacking racks of vials filled with various kinds of seeds and substances in boxes and sending them down in the elevator.

He and his splinter group of post-Volvist neo-Havenites had been collecting genetic material from all the world's species in anticipation of just such an event. Not surprisingly, the prince's followers were more convinced than ever that their leader had been right all along.

Prince Nolan was, of course, thoroughly convinced of his place at the edge of history and seized the moment with fervor. However, not everyone onboard the platform agreed with his tactics.

Chief Scientist Errol Cummings had left on the same boat George came in on. He was one of the lucky ones.

As George heard the noise and felt the impact of the helicopter's crash, he felt particularly unlucky. Not only had both Cummings and the prince himself threatened him with a breach-of-contract lawsuit if he didn't get the machine working properly again, but now he had missed both the boat *and* the helicopter. He had expected to be finished the final recalibrations and runtime tests by now, but the solar storm had been playing hell with his instruments. And now this. He turned off the meter and set aside the probes and looked out the window. Things were much worse that when he had last looked outside. He felt a powerful shudder in the floor beneath him. Probably best to take a look.

George was momentarily dumbfounded at what he saw. Strips of sheet metal and plastic panels flew through the air as the hurricane tore the roofs off both of the new buildings. The first to go was the roof of the casino. The aquatic-themed banners hanging there were ripped from the exposed rafters and a few diehard gamblers scrambled for cover as potted plants and buffet bars were overturned by the winds or swept away entirely. Minutes later, the mounting storm pried its icy fingers under the triangular polyhedra on the windward edge of the roof of the hotel. Section by section, the raging wind tore off and threw down row after row of glasswork. Windows popped and shattered noisily all around.

As the Seahaven platform was buffeted by the huge waves, many onboard scrambled to the steps leading down to the water, some clutching their precious belongings or the hand of a loved one, only to see their hopes of escape dashed as the boats below were smashed against the concrete pylons by battering waves. Seahaven had been far outside the realm of law; now, rescue seemed far outside the realm of hope.

As titanic waves and fierce winds threatened to tear the platform from its footings, it lurched to and fro, pitching items from the deck into the tumultuous sea. Support structures snapped, and one of the six massive support beams below Seahaven buckled. Then, another great wave, and another platform support failed. The deck buckled suddenly as the steel groaned. The whole deck was slipping off its footings!

"This platform is going down," George yelled to the Seahaven staff members crowded near the door of the office. "Where are the life vests?" A woman pointed to a pair of rectangular white storage bins on the deck near the helipad. George struggled against the wind to push open the door. He hurried across the deck to the closest bin, protecting himself from the wind as much as possible. As he opened the bin, the wind caught the lid and yanked it suddenly and forcefully out of his hands. He noticed a woman on the other side of the helipad.

"Help! Please!" she shouted. It was Stevie, the training coordinator.

George grabbed a pair of life vests and made his way to her and helped her put one on. "Stay away from the edges," he advised as he put on the other vest himself. She hung onto one of the supports at the base of the crane and looked up fearfully as lightning flashed in the angry sky.

"I'd be careful of hanging onto anything metallic," George warned her. "We'd be better off inside the building. Come on!" He held her hand and led her to the crowd near the door of the Visitors Centre. There, a team leader was advising people to make their way to the stairs to get to the emergency exit ramps. And there was Chaissie at the back of the line. "You stay with them," shouted George. "Get onto a lifeboat!"

"Where are the lifeboats?" Stevie asked Chaissie.

Chaissie shook her head and pointed to the leeward side of

the platform. "There are no more lifeboats," she said. "Take the exit stairs on this side down to the emergency exit ramps."

"No lifeboats?" Stevie said, incredulously. "What are we supposed to do?"

"Look!" Chaissie cried. "There's Prince Nolan!"

He was at the center of the crowd of Seahaven staff members. "Don't worry—rescuers are on their way," he said, looking confidently to the west.

"I really don't think they will make it in time," warned George. "They can't fly in this weather. It's not safe for helicopters—or rescue ships."

Nolan didn't seem to hear. He kept right on talking.

The lineup Stevie was in was moving slowly toward the stairs. As she neared the edge of the platform, she peered over the edge and watched as a group of panicky people slid down the escape slide. Behind her, the prince was speaking calmly to the people in line through a megaphone. "Believe that you can do it and you will," declared the prince. "Proceed in a calm and orderly fashion. Everything is going to be all right."

As they neared the top of the stairs, Chaissie looked down at the scene of chaos below. She raised her hands in disbelief and frowned. "What? We can't go that way."

"We cannot stay," moaned Stevie, who was right behind her. Stevie saw George looking in their direction and waved to him. He ran over. "Are you coming?" she asked him.

"No. I don't like the look of it. Maybe you should come with me. We'll find another way," he said.

"But this is the way they told us to go," Stevie said. "Down those ramps."

"Those people are probably going to die in that water," warned George, loudly enough that Nolan heard every word.

"Only if they fail to believe they can make it," Nolan challenged him.

"Chaissie!" Nolan called through the megaphone, "Come with me."

Poor Stevie, standing at the top of the stairs, felt caught in the middle. She made her way down the flight of yellow-painted stairs to the ramp and watched as the woman in front of her slid down the long ramp toward the water. Even on the leeward side of the platform, the winds were strong, and the ramp was unstable. The woman made it about halfway down before the buffeting winds threw her off.

Stevie held onto the railing and watched in horror as several other would-be escapees were washed overboard or met similar fates on the flailing ramp. Stevie and several other frightened onlookers stumbled back up the steps, and huddled in the circle of Prince Nolan's followers.

The deck staff continued their efforts to secure the escape ramps and protect their leader; others watched helplessly as their coworkers and members of their community washed overboard. As the platform threatened to capsize, more of the prince's followers panicked and emptied the bins containing the last of the life vests. The prince, sensing their desperation, called for The Kit.

He opened the case, revealing racks of sealed vials of clear red liquid. He held a vial of the liquid aloft before them. "Behold the wine of our redemption. This remarkable liquid," he proclaimed, "is a blood heater that allows you to withstand the cruel, near-freezing temperature of the water." It would, he assured them, allow them the time they would need to withstand the harsh elements until rescue—which he assured them was on the way—arrives. It is safe, he asserted, but only if you take it and, in two minutes, enter the water. Otherwise, he proclaimed, your blood would boil, with catastrophic results. He put his hands on the shoulders of Matt and Stevie. "You two—lead the way. Show them!"

To prove the serum worked, Matt uncapped the vial and gulped down the contents. Nolan then presented a vial to Stevie. She looked uncertain, but Nolan gave her the 'trust me' look and, after a pause, she threw it down, smashing the vial on the metal deck.

"No way," she said. "You can't drink antifreeze. It will cause kidney failure, brain damage, death. Trust me, it just won't work. It's suicide!"

Nolan scowled. "Remember!" he shouted, "The world is watching!"

The groaning of the metal struts and supports grew louder as Nolan bade his followers farewell at the top of the stairs. He took Stevie by the hand and led her back toward the stairs. "Show them the way," he commanded her. "Follow her to safety," he said through the megaphone, as he led her down and onto the slide in a seated position. Another of his followers sat close behind her and clutched her waist, as he pushed them off with a wave. As they slipped down the escape ramp to the water below, Miran watched from the top deck in shock.

Many of the other followers were unsure of what to do

next and tension was high. Those who had taken The Wine watched the clock intently, their fears rising. Sweat beaded up on foreheads. Was it the heat of blood about to boil, or just panic?

Matt came down the slide unevenly and splashed, unconscious, into the water.

Nolan tugged on Chaissie's arm. "This way," he said, and he led her to an unmarked door behind the Visitor Center. He punched in a four-digit code and opened the door. He pushed Chaissie through the door and followed her, pulling the door closed behind him. Inside was an open elevator platform—the type used for moving equipment or supplies. Mounted on the yellow-painted metal grate was a telephone and a set of controls. Nolan punched the green down button and lifted the handset. "We're heading down to S1," he said. "Be ready."

The elevator moved swiftly and noisily, banging and shuddering as it passed down through the levels 4... 3... 2... He pressed a red button and the elevator shuddered to a stop at L1. He slid open the grated metal door. There in front of them was a ramp marked S1 and, at the end of it, a small submarine hanging just above the turbulent surface of the water. "This might be a bit tricky," he said. "Hang on tight."

Chaissie held on to the railing for dear life as the hatch of the sub opened. "Okay. Hang on to me. Let's go." He led her to the open hatch and helped her down into the dark opening. He followed her into the craft and pulled the hatch closed.

"You sit in the back seat—I'll be right there," Nolan said as he sealed the hatch and flipped a set of switches on the interior of the craft. "Strap yourself in!" he yelled. "This is going to be a bit bumpy."

The sub bobbed wildly in the water as he slid into the front seat and tightened his seatbelt. He turned to her. "All buckled in?"

She nodded.

"All right, then—here we go!"

He flipped a switch and a yellow light flashed on and began to rotate. The sound of the winch motor reverberated through the hull as the minisub began to move. Through the large windows, Chaissie could see the cables unspooling as the sub was lowered through the aperture on the lowest deck.

"You said there weren't any boats."

"There must always be an answer," said Nolan as he flipped a switch to disengage the hooks. "Here is ours. It's equipped with the latest in scientific miracles." He turned on the craft's powerful lights, illuminating the deep green water around them.

"Are there more boats?"

He shrugged. "They have their life vests."

Chaissie looked up into the dark structure. Above them, the steel groaned and a third support twisted and broke. The entire platform began to slip sideways into the water. The hooks swung wildly back and forth, clanging against the metal beams on either side of the winch. Nolan blew the ballast tanks and steered the craft nose-first into the churning water.

As the craft moved downward, Chaissie watched in horror from the window as people floundered in the cold water above and around them. The craft struggled against the currents as it lurched past the pylon near the emergency escape steps.

Just as the sub cleared the pylons, the platform's gravity base broke free and the huge platform began to tip—slowly, almost imperceptibly at first—diagonally into the sea. Engines at full, the tiny craft struggled to resist the massive suction as the doomed platform began its slow descent into the watery depths.

* * *

George grabbed Miran's arm and two of the life vests. "Put this on quick. Come on. Follow me. We'll have to jump."

"What?! We're six hundred feet up. We'll drown!"

"No, I mean jump forward."

"There will be lots of floating debris!" she protested. "They've sent distress signals. There will be boats coming. It's safer to take our chances here."

"No way. Not in this storm. I'm jumping." He ran to the wrecked helicopter and grabbed two parachutes. "Come with me!"

The windows in the Visitors Center rattled noisily as George and Miran ran past them toward the room containing the new jump station. George hastily began the jump sequencer.

"Put this on over your life jacket and tighten the straps as much as you can. Be ready to pull this ripcord when I tell you to." The initialization sequence lights began to flash. 3... 2...

"Get ready to pull the cord!" He punched the button. "Now!"

Blink. Suddenly they were gone.

* * *

On the submarine's viewscreen, Prince Nolan and Chaissie watched clouds of bubbles escape as the dark mass slowly descended below the waves. Nolan set the autopilot on and unclipped his seatbelt. He slid out of the chair and squeezed past Chaissie, then opened to door to the cargo bay behind them. The hold was filled with racks of cryotubes and vials filled with seeds, spores, cuttings, and other genetic materials. Nolan checked the straps securing the racks and examined the freezer settings. All good.

Nolan climbed back into the pilot's seat and pulled back on the yoke to level off. As the hydroplanes responded to the controls, he checked the compass and depth gauge, then applied the throttle. The engines hummed a little louder as the sub pushed forward. He barely heard the sounds of the ship, so preoccupied was he with his loss. Behind him, the crane atop the doomed platform was the last part of Seahaven to fall beneath the water's surface. Seahaven had fallen, but the plan had survived.

* * *

Blink. Suddenly the sky was clear and the platform was tipped over, its top section almost completely shorn off. George and Miran were falling.

"*Ahhhh!*"

"*Ahhhhh!!*"

George's red-and-white parachute fluttered above his head then opened. Miran's opened a second later. They drifted away from the broken pylons that remained and splashed down into the water.

"Augh! It's cold!" She saw George struggling with his parachute harness. "Pull that orange tab to inflate your life vest," she shouted.

"Hey! A boat!" They waved their hands frantically.

The boat swung around and reduced its speed. A man on deck shouted to them as they floundered in the cold water. "Ahoy! You look like you could use some help."

"Yes, please," yelled Miran, swimming toward the boat, as a deckhand readied a ladder.

The man surveyed the surrounding area. "Are there just two of you out here?"

"Yes," replied George, tugging Miran closer to the ladder.

"We've got two here," shouted the man and another deckhand rushed over to assist.

"And would your name be George?" asked the man, extending a hand to pull Miran up and onto the deck.

George grabbed a rung of the ladder with nearly numb fingers and began pulling himself out of the water. "That's me."

The two men helped him up the ladder and onto the deck. "There you go. Chilly in there, I bet." He helped them out of their parachute harnesses and life vests as the other man wrapped warm blankets around them and checked them over.

"You don't want to be out in that for too long in these temperatures," he said as he helped them unclip the life preservers. "That's better."

"Yes, thanks."

"Is there anyone or anything else out here we should be looking for?"

"No, just us."

"Well, I hope our services were to your liking today."

"They certainly were. Thank you for the timely pickup."

"We saw the parachutes coming down, just like you said."

"How... did you arrange that?"

"I had one of my agents take care of it."

* * *

Miran had plenty of time to think on the long trip back. She wasn't sure what she wanted to do. She knew what she didn't want, though. She never wanted to see that cruel and callous man again—the bastard who had left her to die on that old sea-relic. She was glad her daughter hadn't been there to see that.

It was bad enough that they'd been banished from Haven by Nolan's father, ashamed that his son should be consorting with the likes of her. But Nolan behaving the same way when she declined to get 'aug'ed with him—well, that was a burn that really left a mark. Such hypocrisy!

Her resentment welled up inside like poison in the bloodstream. Best to think of something else.

"What are *you* planning to do?" she asked George as the boat sped toward the mainland.

"I am going home for a while. Home to my old condo in Princeton. I'm going to do a whole lotta nothing for a while. You're welcome to come with me if you need a place to stay for a while."

"I haven't decided yet. I'm still a bit shaken up."

"Almost dying will do that to you."

"You're planning to see your daughter, aren't you?"

Miran nodded. "If I can find her."

"Listen, why don't you come with me? We'll go to the old lab and I can help you find her. In fact, I'll bet you Kaedra knows where she is. We can ask her."

"Oh, she doesn't want to see me. I'm her son's ex."

"I don't know much about how she cares about that. But I'll bet she cares about her only grandchild."

"I suppose. Wait, no. I can't go back there. I've been expelled. Banned for life."

"Oh, right. Well maybe I can invite her out for an afternoon. She did say she wanted to go out on a walk with me. That might be a good time to talk to her."

"I don't know. She'd probably tell Saros. Or Nolan. I never want to see either one of those two so-and-sos ever again."

"I understand. Anyway, this is not all about them, it's about you and what *you* want. You want to see your daughter, don't you?"

She nodded.

"Well, I'll bet she will be delighted to see you, too. That's something to look forward to. Last time I saw Frigg, she was working in the same lab I was. She was doing really well. How long has it been since you've seen her?"

"Oh, must be at least seven years. She was just a kid. She never came out to Seahaven."

"Well, we can set that right pretty easily. We'll go to her."

"The woman who's the head of Frigg's department is a friend of mine. And I'd be pleased to be able to help a little with that."

"Wait a minute—how was she working in the same lab as you? Weren't you working for Isaac Stern?"

"Yeah, but she worked there after he passed away."

"So, she was there when Andrew owned the place, then?"

George nodded.

She looked incredulous. "He wouldn't have allowed her anywhere near him. He banned our whole family from the place forever."

"Well, I don't know exactly who hired her or why, but I can tell you, (a) she's a pretty good lab assistant, and (b), the hiring policies around that lab have absolutely nothing to do with the color of a person's skin or anything else. If they've got the skills, they've got a shot at a career there. Andrew Stern isn't the hiring authority there, anyway. There's an HR department for that."

"That sounds like an improvement from the time I knew him."

"I'm not defending him, and we've certainly had our disagreements over the years. But Frigg has done well on her own merits—no one else's. I doubt that anyone there even knows she's related to Andrew Stern."

"He'd certainly never mention it," Miran said. "And I doubt my ex would, either."

Five days later, the mainland was finally in sight. That afternoon, the boat docked at the marina on the mainland south of Gull Island. It had been a 1308-mile trip in all.

Miran had proven to be a pleasant traveling companion and something of an expert on aquatic birds. George had impressed her, though, when he was able to correctly identify a Storm Petrel by its original colonial name.

Of course, the trip would have been much faster if they'd taken a helicopter—or even a boat—to St. Johns, Newfoundland and then taken a plane from there back to New Jersey. But George had come to realize that, when it seems like you have all the time in the world, sometimes spending a little of it doing something you enjoy is its own reward.

* * *

15

Retrospective

From the Archives: Oct 19, 2051

"Welcome back to *Retrospective*. I'm Dorine Kwan. Today we're taking a look at the life and legacy of bioengineering and Genetech pioneer Isaac Stern and the rise and fall of the Andna Corporation, Stern's ill-fated business empire.

"We begin with this extraordinary excerpt from a June 6, 2039 interview with senior researcher and former director of the research facility that gave birth to Andna Corporation, Dr. Jonathon Majors."

"I remember the day they called me into the Dean's office and Isaac Stern was sitting there. He'd convinced them that my dedication to our core mission somehow meant I had no vision, didn't take direction well, and so on.

"It's true that I had been critical of Stern's call for a new approach to some of the challenges we were facing at the time, but I didn't expect him to go behind my back by secretly meeting with the board of directors of the science committee to discuss the issue.

"I was eligible for a paid sabbatical at the time, so they positioned the proposition as 'let's have Isaac run the show for that twelve-month period.' So, they appointed Isaac Stern as interim director, quote-unquote. And they promised to do a formal evaluation in twelve months' time. I guess my agreement to that was my big mistake.

"I tried arguing that we were too close to cracking the big field equations we'd been pursuing. We were so close. I knew that Emil Fidor at CERN was particularly close to solving the problem; I felt quite strongly that we would be forfeiting our advantage if I stepped down. I made a stand and said I wouldn't go.

"But they said: 'Sorry, Jonathon. If you don't take the sabbatical, we're taking you off the project anyway.' So, that was that."

"So," said Dorine, "you must have felt resentful of Isaac Stern. Did you feel as though your legacy was at risk?"

"Sure, I was resentful of Isaac Stern. We didn't think too much about legacy, really—we were more focused on keeping the momentum of the research program going. I had to watch as the organization I helped build was steered off-course by straying too much from our core mission, which was to be a leader in the field of high energy large accelerators.

"Isaac Stern was fairly notorious for commercializing student-led innovations and then cutting them out of the profit picture.

"Stern's willingness to patent technologies developed by

the school's own graduate students was, in my mind, reprehensible. He built a multibillion-dollar business empire by exploiting their naïvety; he simply didn't treat his top people fairly.

"Prior to Stern taking over the organization—initially as interim director, and later as CEO—we worked closely with partners such as CERN and the Brookhaven institute. We partnered with thought leaders like Doctors Emil Fidor and Eldon Johnson—very smart folks I continue to work with today. Isaac was willing to burn those bridges in an attempt to corner the market—they'd say they were *disrupting* the market—to gain a competitive advantage.

"A prime example of that attitude was the commercialization of the Princeton Deep Learning project into a business. First, it was marketed as 'business AI,' then 'Xavier,' which was a bit of a joke around the research community, where everyone was calling it the 'hack savior.' They spun off an enterprise edition as a paid product; it then became a subscription— 'software as a service.' And then, rumor has it, they somehow convinced the government to pay for it all over again, as a military automation solution called ADA. And if that wasn't enough, they later repackaged the Savi front-end together with the old XAVR backend and called *that* 'Anna.' So, quite a lot of repackaging, there. The running joke around the academic community was that Stern's patent holding company, AIMG, stood for Artificial Intelligence Marketing Gimmicks, which honestly, is not far from the truth."

"In fact," said Dorine Kwan, "AIMG stood for Advanced Innovations Marketing Group. It was, by most accounts, a patent holding company with only one purpose: to aggressively seek to enforce patent rights through litigation or threats of litigation. Such companies are commonly referred to as patent assertion entities, or more pejoratively, as patent trolls."

Majors shrugged. "That's how it seemed. But they kept pivoting, and they kept growing. By 2030, AIMG was making so much money through patent litigation, the people working for Stern's company had little incentive to produce anything themselves.

"Details of what happened next are sketchy, but it is known that the hiring of Dr. Erich Rössler and a team of engineers, programmers, and mathematicians led, less than a year later, to a major breakthrough that caught the attention of the U.S. military and led to contracts rumored to be worth more than thirty-two billion dollars."

"That kind of year-over-year growth," said Dr. Majors, "was truly remarkable for a company valued at an estimated six hundred million dollars only a year earlier. But one can't help but wonder what was worth that much money to the U.S. military.

"Investor interest was fueled by rumors that the company had achieved—or was about to achieve—some sort of breakthrough on a technology that, it was said, equaled the atomic bomb in its strategic potential. Speculators saw these activities as a sure sign that the company was on the verge of some sort of major breakthrough. There were rumors that they had achieved some sort of major advance—not just theoretical physics—but something really new, involving new quantum states of energy, space and time; rumors of the development of some sort of time machine were bolstered by the presence of renowned space-time theorist Dr. Eldon Johnson at the company's secretive tech summit.

"Such extraordinary growth did not come without consequences, however. Isaac's marriage to his first wife Caroline crumbled as the company rapidly diversified into biotech, AI, and other areas where its technological leadership was not as assured."

"I was working at the Brookhaven National Laboratory at the time," said Dr. Majors. "We experienced the disruptive influence of those new ventures, but perhaps not in the way that our competitor expected. Initially, MPAX—that was what Stern's company was calling itself at the time—was perceived as a segment leader. Everyone on the investor circuit wanted to know if we had a competitive offering to this-or-that product in their lineup. At the time, we were very focused on nuclear and particle physics and things like nanomaterials research. Suddenly, we were being asked what *we* were doing in quantum field effects research, high-energy light acceleration and related photon sciences, and all of the other areas that perhaps it looked as though Isaac's company was no longer focusing on. And then, when their board of directors made the decision to appoint an artificial intelligence as CEO of the company, which then changed the company name and mission statement *again*, well, no one knew quite what to think about that. It just seemed crazy at the time.

"But, then, as decentralized autonomous orgs became more commonplace, the investors warmed up to the idea and the next thing you know, their stock was doing well again. I suppose that when Andna moved away from its roots in quantum physics research and into chasing the next big thing, with all the biotech stuff, that was when the investors really began to lose confidence."

Kwan's voice-over narration continued. "That loss of confidence was exacerbated by several contributing factors during the period leading up to the summer of 2037: Isaac Stern suffered multiple personal and business setbacks during this period. A major government contract went sour, allegedly over accusations that top-secret code had been leaked by Andna employees. This was followed by not one but two terrorist attacks that culminated in the theft of top-secret military prototype technology rumored to be worth more than thirty billion dollars. Isaac Stern died that same summer, in circumstances that remain controversial.

"The final blow, some say, was the havoc that occurred in January 2038, when automated systems worldwide went down all at once during the most notorious and damaging hack attack in recorded history, now referred to the Omega Event. In just eight seconds, it paralyzed network and internet-connected systems worldwide—especially organizations as dependent as they were on machine intelligence and ubiquitous connectivity as Andna was at the time.

"By the end of 2038, employees at the company were hit with a wide-ranging round of layoffs. Planned expansions were cancelled and Andna stock plummeted to an historic low.

"The troubled organization's next phase began when NASA—perhaps enticed by the prospect of picking up some of Andna's leading-edge tech at fire-sale prices—made a play for some of Andna's key assets, including its patent portfolio and members of its core development and engineering teams.

"One of the technologies NASA was particularly interested in was an innovative communications system that, it was claimed, allowed virtually instantaneous communications over great distances via entangled 'qubits.' NASA hoped to exploit this so-called 'Qmunications' technology in aid of the president's stated goal of landing an American on a planet in a different solar system by the end of the century. However, it seems fate had other ideas.

"NASA's Alan Hull explains: 'The space race more or less ended with the loss of American lives on Mars and on the Boca Chica launchpad in 2050.' At that point, China, India, and Russia were all focusing more on robotic missions anyway; the dream of sending humans on high-risk missions into deep space just didn't seem to make much sense anymore."

"There was, however, increasing amounts of evidence that NASA was on the verge of a big breakthrough."

The interviewer helped an uncomfortable-looking Alan Hull adjust his lapel microphone. "Camera in 3 ... 2 ..."

"Yeah, I worked with a guy named George Gunderson, who said he was able to supply us with a working time machine. We worked together on a system that could be implemented aboard a moving spacecraft."

"The effort, known as Project Starjumper, appears to have been a success. Gunderson himself was absent from all records for eight years, lending credibility to reports that he personally tested the alleged time-displacement device.

"Another person with a propensity to disappear for extended periods of time was Isaac Stern's own son, Andrew, who was reported to frequently disappear for days or weeks at a time during the eleven-year period following the Omega Event in January 2038.

"*Retrospective* spoke to Marcie Morgan, a former girlfriend of Andrew's."

"I knew Andrew Stern and his father, sure. I introduced him to my friends in the summer of... I wanna say 2036? Anyway, we went out that summer. I had no idea he was so rich. He was kinda strange, though.

"What was interesting was when I ran into him again in 2051. He had barely aged a day. He looked just like he did 15 years earlier. We should all be so lucky."

"Around this time, Andrew Stern became a member of the board of directors of Andna Corporation and a governance committee that, in cooperation with the European Organisation for Nuclear Research, announced an international non-military fundamental research project, dubbed EON Research. This scientific consortium was where Andrew Stern met his future wife, Dr. Marjorie Blint, and the famed astrophysicist and occasional astronaut Dr. Emil Fidor—both of whom would later disappear under mysterious circumstances."

"Coming up on *Retrospective*: A new Space-Time division at NASA leads to mysterious missives from the future and heartbreak for Andrew Stern."

* * *

16

Ad Astra

2043

The receptionist put down the phone receiver. "You can go in now."

Mark Banyan, the ASTRA program director, extended his hand. "Hello Marjorie. Thanks for coming in today. And you must be Andrew. A pleasure. Please have a seat. I understand you two recently got married? Congrats."

The director sat down behind his desk. "Thank you, Andrew, for all the work that you and your team have done for NASA. The whole ASTRA division is indebted to the work that your father started and you and the other fine people at Andna have carried through to fruition. As you may know, we're getting close to the testing phase for project Starjumper and, well, that's why I wanted to chat with you.

"As you're probably aware, there's a fairly limited group of people inside and outside of the org who are aware of what we're trying to do here and, frankly, we'd like to keep it that way. Given that that the two of you have both the necessary top-secret clearance and the skill profiles we need for this mission, I wanted to see if you're interested in participating.

"There will, of course, be some pretty intensive training, as Marjorie already knows, and we'll have to have a few other people in training as backups, but I think I can get you two onto a very short list for a mission in 2045, if you're up for it. What do you think?"

"It's an honor to be considered for a mission with the potential of such historic significance. I will let Marjorie speak for herself, but I can say I'm looking forward to doing everything I can to make this mission a great success, sir."

"That's all we can hope for, thank you. Marjorie?"

"As you know, sir, I'm delighted to be on the candidate list, and I share Andrew's enthusiasm for this project and look forward to a successful outcome. Can you give us a little more of an idea about the mission goals and parameters?"

"We're still working out the exact details, but we have a few things we know for sure we'd like to accomplish: Number one, we want to send you around to the other side of the moon and turn on the Starjumper for a couple of short-term tests, to evaluate our ability to successfully displace a stationary object with the temporal field effect, and then to try the same thing with a moving object. We've seen static co-ordinate-based jumps working well down here, we just want to be sure it works with our space-based portable equipment. And, conversely, we've never had much success with temporal manipulation of moving objects down here in a gravity-based environment, but we'd like to verify that the behavior is the same out there in zero-G space.

"And, assuming we get at least one of those results going in the right direction, our second test will be little more exciting. We've got this idea to try to keep a mouse alive out there in a mini-spacepod, then run the pod through the Starjumper set for something spectacularly longer than a mouse's normal lifespan, like ten years. Then, we'll see if the little guy is still alive. We want to understand if we can use this tech to send people out there into space for long-term missions that would otherwise be beyond our lifespan to, you know, really get way out there."

"Sounds exciting."

"Yes, well, we're going to need that kind of capability if we're ever hoping to make it to the stars. Hence our motto: *sic itur ad astra*."

* * *

The preflight test regimen was more challenging than Andrew had expected it to be. He handled the math, space science, and physics portions of the written tests with aplomb, but was very nearly sidelined when the doctors saw his prematurely aged right hand—the result of an accident while testing an early version of the 'bubble within a bubble' technology of the prototype Bubblecraft, back in 2034.

Fortunately, his hand and arm strength were not unduly compromised by the accident, and he managed to complete all of the survival training and physical endurance tests required, as did Marjorie.

24 months later, Andrew completed the training program with honors and joined Marjorie on the flight roster for NASA's first ion-propulsion-based spacecraft, dubbed the Aion-1, slated to lift off in August, to coincide with the period when the moon is closer to Earth than usual, known as its perigee—August 12th marked the moon's closest approach to our planet. If, for some reason, that launch window was missed, they'd have to wait until the next perigee period.

In mid-June, while the two of them were in the waiting queue, rumors began to circulate that changes in the program were imminent. Unspecified changes seldom meant good news.

"I swear, if they cancel our flight, I will hit the roof," vowed Marjorie. She held Andrew's left hand. "You've worked so hard for this."

* * *

As is often the case, NASA's original Aion-1 launch-date estimates slipped a few times due to various technical snags. Most of the issues were related to the ion propulsion system, not the Starjumper tech. The original two-year 'best case' estimate had fallen apart while Andrew and Marjorie were still in training. But the mission plan had always been to train them early and then jump them forward when the tech was ready for them. And, to maximize the positive PR potential of the news coverage, the plan had always been for Marjorie to lead the mission. As the only one on the mission with prior orbital experience, Marjorie had a head start on the pre-flight portion of the training program. When the mission planners suggested that she jump ahead to meet Andrew's completion date, she agreed.

That was when everything went wrong.

* * *

NASA's new psyche profiling algorithm decided that the best chance for meeting the mission objectives would be have Marjorie jump forward to provide the best possible outcome in mutual mental readiness for the upcoming mission.

"Andrew's estimated completion date is 16 days from now," the mission advisory told her. She would be jumping forward a little less than sixteen days to be ready when he was and sync up with him. "We'll be using the ground-based jump platform," they explained as they prepped the transit platform for the 380-hour jump. The newly upgraded jump platform had been mentioned during her training, but this was the first time she'd seen it in action. The movement of the transit pods was now completely automated. It was a huge improvement over the previous-generation jumpstation setups she was familiar with. Now, there was virtually no way for an unexpected intersection collision to occur. That was a welcome change from the old system where the technicians —or sometimes even the jumper herself—had to manually drag the pod off the platform in five minutes or less, or else risk an intersection event. This looked much safer. Or so she thought.

Strapped into the pod, she listened to the final countdown to the jump. Three ... two ... one ...

Blink.

380 hours later, the jump platform crew was surprised when absolutely nothing appeared on the receiving end of the jump. There wasn't even a "jump successful" status message. That was worrying.

The platform manager immediately called the mission controller. "We have a negative condition on post-jump status report and nothing to show here. Pod did not appear. I repeat: the pod did *not* appear. We're investigating now."

"Roger that." Keep us informed."

The platform manager walked briskly over to the control desk and spoke to the technician there. "Any ideas?"

"No ma'am," he said. "Everything looked AOK prior to the jump. I'm running a diagnostic.... Wait—oh, this is bad." He pointed to a line in the diagnostic data marked as ERROR. "Look, there is a failover event that starts here. For some reason, it couldn't complete the primary jump routine and passed it over to the failover routine. Hmm." He pondered the code for a moment.

The manager knew how it was supposed to work. "... Which should have retried and then, if necessary, transferred control to the failsafe jump routine. And if *that* failed, it should have just errored out and ended with a status message. So where was that?"

"We had a secondary jump target set slightly earlier than the original target, as usual. Says here the secondary target for this one was configured for 15.625 days. That's 375 hours. So, clearly that one didn't happen, either."

"Get some eyes on that failover code," barked Program

Director Banyan. "I want to know what kind of problem we're dealing with here."

Four hours later...

A software engineer raised his arm. "I've got it."

"You found something, Allan?"

"Yep. It's the failover jump subroutine that takes our primary jump (hours) parameter—in our case, that's the 380-hour value—and looks up the nearest failover value, which is in hours down here, where it says 375."

Yeah, I see that."

"So far so good. But look what happens next: that routine looks up the 375-hour value and plugs it into the secondary jump routine. And there's your problem. It's falling through to a routine that parses the value and uses it to set the jump value. But that value isn't being initialized properly. So, it is getting a null value, which in this code is equivalent to years. All the other values are fractional values of that default value."

"What!?"

"Yeah, it's converting to years, not hours."

"So, we sent her forward 375 *years* instead of 375 hours? Oh, crap. And how did we miss that?"

"It looks like... yeah, I see the problem now. If the tested value is years, days, minutes or seconds, the jumps in the code and the routine that converts everything down to seconds work correctly. But if the value is expressed in hours..."

"... it's falling through to years."

"Yep. My guess is that whoever tested the failover code tested for seconds, minutes, days, and years—all of which would have tested correctly. Maybe they just assumed that hours worked, too. Or maybe they just missed that test. It's normally unexecuted code, so there haven't been many cases when it gets called at all."

"And we still don't know what caused the initial error condition?"

"No. But it could've been something like a solar flare. A big solar storm would do it. All it would take would be for cosmic rays or whatever to just flip a couple of bits so that the checksum doesn't match and—boom—you'd hit this code."

"All right, good work, Allan Get that code fixed ASAP, will you please? And get someone to look into space weather conditions and other possible corollaries that might have caused that error. I've got some explaining to do to the folks upstairs."

* * *

Andrew leaned close to the microphone stalk protruding from the command console. "This is Aion-1 calling mission control, over."

"This is mission control. What's going on up there? Over."

"Everything is fine. I think I *might* have stumbled across the reason the moving target tests are always a little bit off. Over."

"Do tell. Over."

"As you know, we are using magnetospheric sync signals to lock onto. But they are always offset. I was comparing the magnetospheric data and the displacement vector plotting data and, correct me if I'm wrong, but it doesn't look like we are compensating for the magnetic field streamlines caused by the Sun's rotation—you know, the Parker spiral effect. Can you guys look into that?"

"Roger that, Aion-1. We'll investigate and get back to you on that *asap*. Over."

Four hours later, mission control called again. "Good news, Andrew. Your hunch has checked out. Our engineers think we may be able to compensate for the Parker spiral effect by utilizing a couple of rotating Helmholtz coils. You've got them rather excited by the possibility of a good solution to this long-standing issue. Well done. Over."

"Well, compensating for the effect is definitely not going to be a trivial task. The magnetic streamline values are highly dynamic, so the calculations will vary, depending on the relationship between the radial velocity of the solar wind and the magnetic field, angle of rotation, and so on. So, lots to do there, I'm sure. But I'm glad I was able to point them in the right direction, over."

"Well, we sure appreciate it. Over."

"Aion-1, over and out."

* * *

"What are we going to tell Andrew?" asked the jump steward.

"Don't jeopardize the mission until we know what the hell the plan is."

17

The Well-Dressed Man

2436

George's phone buzzed. He didn't recognize the number, but it was a long one. "Hello?"

"Hello. I'm calling for George Gunderson."

"This is he. How can I help you?"

"I understand you are an expert in an area of interest to my employer. We have need of your services and will pay your way here for a meeting to discuss the matter further."

"I only fly first class," fibbed George.

"Of course. First class. Will you be needing one ticket or two?"

"Two, please. May I ask where exactly are you?"

"China. Are you available to fly out tomorrow and stay as our guest for the weekend? All expenses paid."

"That sounds just fine."

"The details will be sent with your itinerary. Are you still at your address in Skyscraper Shadows?"

"Yes, that will be fine. And may I ask to whom I am speaking?"

"My name is Viktor; I am calling on behalf of Mr. Thom. It is he with whom you will be meeting."

"I'm looking forward to it."

"As are we. A detailed itinerary is on its way to you now."

"Thank you."

"Thank *you*, sir. Good day."

And that was that.

"Hey Surya. Are you busy tomorrow?"

"I might be. What's up?"

"Would you like to come along on a nice all-expenses-paid vaycay and fly first-class to... oh, I don't know, somewhere exotic?"

"Sounds terrible. Yeah, I might be interested. Does it have to be tomorrow?"

"Well, it's actually for the whole weekend, but, yeah, we'd have to leave tomorrow."

"What are you not telling me about this? What's the catch?"

George wondered the same thing, but he didn't see any obvious red flags.

"I just got off the phone with the representative for the people we'll be meeting and, while I don't know this person, he just sent me the plane tickets. I checked them out. They are indeed first class and they are legit; departure time is 12 noon tomorrow."

"And how long is the flight?"

"Oh, it's long all right."

"You guys always say that," she said with a wink.

"No really, it's a 17-hour flight."

"Seventeen?! Good grief! How many stops?"

"That's the thing. Seventeen hours with no stops."

"Yikes. Where is this place—on the other side of the world?"

"Pretty much. I hope you like Chinese food."

"China?! Well, I'll be sure to bring my red shoes. I've always wanted to go there."

"Well tomorrow's your lucky day, then. I recommend overdressing for this one, okay?"

"Oh, I get to see you dressed up again? Good stuff. All right, I'll come over as soon as I finish packing. Bye."

* * *

The next day...

Just after 9 a.m., a courier knocked on the door and handed George a small package. Inside was a folder with a detailed itinerary and an envelope containing five hundred dollars in cash and a handwritten note. *Please take a taxi to the airport,* it said. *Transportation will be provided from there.*

* * *

Seventeen-hour nonstop flights are, by their very nature, terribly boring, but if you have to do it, Surya decided, first class was definitely the way to go. Great food, luxurious blankets, comfortable seats with lots of legroom—even the Champagne was decent.

When George and Surya stepped off the plane and made

their way through customs, a man with a card saying 'George G' flagged them down and directed them to a waiting limousine. It was just after 11 a.m., Beijing time.

"This is very posh, isn't it?" whispered Surya as the car sped along the S51 Airport Expressway.

"It says here we'll be staying at the Ritan Hotel overlooking Ritan Park and the Temple of the Sun. Five-star hotel, apparently."

"Sounds sunny-delightful."

As the driver unloaded their luggage from the trunk, Viktor opened their door and handed them both an envelope.

"Compliments of Mister Thom," he said. "Please do not be late for the scheduled meetings. You received the itinerary, I trust?"

"Yes, thank you."

"I will accompany you to the hotel reception desk to ensure that all the arrangements are as they should be.

Please follow me."

Surya snuck a look inside the envelope as they walked. Inside was a handwritten note that said:

You will find that the Silk Market is not far from the hotel if you like to do some shopping. Here is a credit card for each of you for your expenses. Please keep your receipts.

Viktor closed the car door behind them. "Please be back here at the hotel by six o'clock local time for dinner as guests of Mister Thom." He looked at his obviously expensive watch. "That is exactly five hours and forty-five minutes from now. Please follow me."

George wondered if it was a coincidence that Viktor spoke English with a vaguely Russian-sounding accent and the hotel was in the area of Beijing commonly known as 'the Russian quarter.' Russian Mafia, perhaps?

Viktor spoke to the desk clerk in Russian. "Привет. У меня есть Джордж Гундерсон и его гость, чтобы они заселились, пожалуйста."

George's phone translated the exchange. "Hello. I have George Gunderson and his guest to check in, please."

The receptionist smiled. "Все в порядке. Вот ключи от комнаты. Спасибо," she replied as she handed him two small packets.

"All is well. Here are the keys to the room. Thank you," said George's translator.

Viktor turned to George and Surya. "Here are your room keys. They speak passably good English at the concierge desk, over there. And you have my number if you encounter any problems. I'll meet you here at 6 p.m. sharp."

"We'll be here—thank you," said George.

Viktor turned and walked toward the lobby doors.

When he was out of sight, Surya grinned and showed George the credit card.

"Now you're looking dangerous," he said with a smile.

"Let's look at the room," suggested Surya. "Did we get one room or two?"

George pushed the elevator button and looked at the folder containing the keycard.

"I don't know. Mine says room 505. What about yours?"

"Same."

The elevator doors opened on the fifth floor. "503, 504, ah, here it is." She slid her keycard into the door lock and pushed the door open.

"Ah, two beds. Maybe I'll share mine if you're extra nice to me."

"Or, hey, why don't you just push 'em together and we'll use both of them?"

"So, who is this Thom guy, anyway? He must be pretty rich."

"I don't know for sure, but I have a feeling this is related to the stuff we did at Andna. Maybe they want to build a jumpstation here. It has to be something pretty big."

"Mm, comfy bed."

"You want to go shopping?"

She unbuttoned her blouse. "I dunno. What are you selling? Wait, let me guess: Something pretty big."

"*You* are a mind reader."

* * *

George straightened his cufflinks as Surya put on a necklace. "It's two minutes to six," he said.

"Don't worry. I'll be ready in a minute. It only takes a minute to get there. We'll be there on time." She snapped her purse closed. "Okay, I'm ready."

At 6 p.m. sharp, the elevator door opened and Surya, wearing a spectacular red evening gown and George, wearing a black tux, stepped into the lobby.

Viktor was already there, checking his watch. "Ah, right on time," he said. "This way, please."

"Mister Thom will be joining us later, after dinner. Please enjoy our hospitality and allow me to introduce you to Emil, who will brief you on our, ah, situation."

Emil was a distinguished looking older man, about 70 years old by George's estimate. He greeted them graciously. "It is a pleasure to meet you, Mister Gunderson. I am familiar with some of your work. Very impressive."

"Why, thank you."

"And this is...?"

"Pardon my manners. This is Surya."

"Surya Byrne. Pleased to meet you."

"Usually, we have servers here to pour the wine, but I thought it might be nice for this meeting to be a little more private, while we're getting to know each other."

Emil gestured towards the wine bottles on the table.

"May I pour either of you a glass of wine? We have a lovely Cabernet here, and also a Riesling white. They're both very good."

Surya nodded. "White for me, please."

"I'll have the same," said George. "Thank you."

Surya took a sip. "Splendid."

Emil poured himself a glass of the red wine. "The food will be coming along very shortly. I'm you both must very hungry and probably very tired after that long flight, so I'll get right to the point. My dear Ms. Byrne, would you be so kind as to allow me to have a private word with George on a matter of some sensitivity? We'll just be a moment, and then we'll have right back for that lovely dinner I've promised you."

"Certainly. Take your time. I'll be in the hall."

"Thank you so much."

Emil stood close to George and spoke in a quiet voice. "I'm sorry, I should have asked earlier. Forgive me for being blunt, but does your friend Surya know anything about your work on all that time-travel stuff? I don't want to place you into an embarrassing situation of having to explain, you know, jumpgates and top-secret military contracts and all that."

George regarded him suspiciously.

"Yes, yes," said Emil, "we know about that, too."

"She knows about the non-military stuff," confirmed George. "She is aware of the non-military work we did at Andna. She was an intern there, back in the early days of the project, and then she did some research work with me where she and I jumped a few hundred years ahead—and she ended up getting an oceanography degree and a position on a research vessel."

"Hm. That's challenging for a jumper."

"So, she worked on those projects, but has never been exposed to any of the military aspects or any of the work that's been done for other parties."

"And would you prefer that we keep it that way?"

"No, I think she could be quite useful. She's very trustworthy and a talented researcher. She has certainly helped me out in the past. I can step outside and ask her if she'd be willing to sign a non-disclosure agreement form, if you'd like."

"If you think she wouldn't mind, yes, please do."

"She'd much rather be included in the discussions, I can assure you."

"Yes, an admirable trait. I have an NDA form right here that Ms. Byrne can sign whenever she's ready."

"I'll go have a brief chat with her. She's signed NDAs before, so ... I'll be right back."

George stood up and headed for the door.

"Hey Surya, sorry for the delay."

"What's going on?"

"Um, there's some sensitive information that they want to disclose to us, but they require us to sign an NDA. Are you okay with that?"

"Does it limit my ability to work on other stuff or affect any other pre-existing knowledge I may have?"

"Nope. It's just their business they don't want us to disclose to others."

"Fine. I'll sign. And then we eat, right? I'm starving."

"Me too. I'll ask them to get the food happening."

"Where do I sign?" she asked Emil.

"Initial here to say that you've read this bit, and then sign there."

"Done and done," said Surya, putting down the pen. "Mm, I smell something good."

Just then, a pair of servers arrived and announced the choices for the first course of the meal. The hors d'oeuvres were followed by a choice of appetizer, the main course, and three kinds of dessert.

After they had all finished their meals and desserts, Emil

signaled to the servers. "That will be all, thank you," he said quietly. They bowed and closed the door to the room.

"There's just a little more business that we can now speak about freely, and we'll be done for tonight. To come straight to the point: We have a jumpstation here, George, that needs a little TLC, as they say."

"You have a jumpstation here? Is it working?"

"Well, not to put too fine a point on it but, that's why we've asked you here. Something's gone wrong—it's probably something quite minor, but we can't seem to isolate the problem."

"I'm very curious, and I'm sure you can imagine why."

"You're curious as to how we have managed to come into the possession of a device that is considered top secret."

"Well, yes, there's that. But also, how you even know how to operate the software, initialize the firmware, all of that. It's remarkable that you were able to do anything with it, frankly."

"Let's just say that it's been a personal goal of mine. What do you Americans call it again? A bucket-list item, yes, that's it. This has been on my bucket list for a very long time. I used to work at CERN, you know."

"You must have known Dr. Fidor, then?"

"Oh yes, I knew him all right. In fact, I am him."

"No. *You're* Dr. Emil Fidor?"

"That's me."

"It's an honor."

"On the contrary, the honor is mine. I would have liked to invite Ms. Everett and the others on your remarkable team here as well, but alas, their areas of expertise seem to reside elsewhere and, well, I don't think your Dr. Rössler would think very kindly of his staff working with a backup copy of his top-secret project. That would be *your* backup copy, as I understand it."

"I see."

"If you'll forgive an old man rambling on about the old days, I can tell you that it had been a dream of mine for many decades to achieve results like yours. I had almost given up hope when we heard rumors that, well, you and the others on Erich Rössler's team had succeeded in solved a problem that had, I'm afraid, always eluded my best efforts. But the mere fact that it is working gives me the greatest sense of satisfaction that my efforts were not completely in vain. What you and your cohorts have achieved is wonderful. It's what I always dreamed of being able to do. So, I approached Mister Thom about recreating this great achievement of yours and, well, we were lucky enough to be able to make it happen, thanks to that firmware and the runtime executive in your backup. That was the missing link, you might say."

"Do you happen to know what revision it is?"

"Oh yes. V2.03."

George nodded. Not a bad version to work with. That was the same one the military started with.

He thought about it a little more. Hmm. That was the version he had installed on the system at Seahaven, too.

"I thought we were going to be meeting with Mister Thom tonight after dinner."

"Ah, yes, he realizes you must be very tired and he suggested that tomorrow's breakfast meeting might be a better time to continue our conversation."

"I'm not sure about you, Surya, but I am feeling a bit jetlagged, I must admit."

"Tomorrow morning is fine with me," she said.

Fidor looked at the message on his commlink.

Haven't received adequate intel on Surya Byrne yet. Stall them.

"Well," he said. "I hope your dinner was enjoyable. We'll try our best to keep the other itinerary items on schedule. See you here in this room for breakfast at 9 a.m. sharp."

* * *

On the way back to their room, Surya asked, "What's the deal with Dr. Fidor? How do you know him?"

He was a pioneer in a lot of the early research that we based our original HELX accelerator design on. Kind of a personal hero of mine, you might say," George said as the elevator doors opened at the fifth floor. "The intriguing thing about Emil Fidor is that he was reported dead. And then, almost 400 years later, he reappears—alive."

"He obviously had access to a jumpgate."

"Yes, but that's interesting, too: there were no records in any of our systems of him or his jumps from that era. Things were pretty easy to look up in those days, as there weren't many IDs or records to go through. So, he must have been using a system we had no record of at Andna."

George skipped the part where he theorized that it might have been a military system.

"He looks to be about seventy," Surya noted, as George unlocked the door to their room. "How old was he when you knew him?"

"Oh, he was the wunderkind genius guy at CERN back in the early 2000s. I guess he would have been about 22 then. It's weird to think that he and I would have been roughly the same age if not for jump tech."

"I'm glad you jumped ahead. God, I was just a kid when I met you."

George took off his tux jacket. "I remember that hairdo you had."

"You liked it?"

George shrugged playfully.

"Come on—that was an awesome hairdo."

"You looked fantastic tonight, by the way," George said as he loosened his tie.

"Would you unzip me?"

* * *

Later...

Surya flipped through the available TV channels. In addition to the Chinese language programming, there were a few Russian and English channels. Curious, she stopped on what appeared to be a news program—or perhaps some sort of strange late-night talk show—with one striking difference: the figure on the screen was shown only as a silhouette on a turquoise background. You couldn't see his face at all. The camera panned over what appeared to be a live studio audience, applauding wildly, as an animated title appeared on the screen. "The Tangler", it said.

Intrigued, Surya unmuted the sound.

"And now, here he is, your host with the most Good News Tomorrow... Ty Thom, The Tangler!"

"Hey, here's a guy with the same last name as your Mister Thom. Do you think that's the guy?"

"Probably just a weird coincidence."

She muted the sound again and leaned over to kiss George. Behind them, the captions showed what was being said by the silhouetted figure.

"Good News Tomorrow: Xin Xin, the giant panda at the Beijing Zoo, will give birth to a cub weighing 130 grams."

* * *

18

The Tangler

Click.

"Today, I'm pleased to introduce a very special guest. He's the mysterious man who's bringing a new type of 'silhoueti-quette' to the daily news. Please give a warm welcome to the host with the most Good News Tomorrow... Ty Thom, The Tangler!"

The audience applauded enthusiastically as the lights came up on a man's silhouetted figure on a bright turquoise background. "Good morning, Mary," said the dark figure. "Thank you for having on your show. It's great to be here."

"You're having quite a year. Good News Tomorrow is now the number one entertainment news program in the UK, Canada and Japan, and you've recently signed a streaming deal for distribution in 26 countries in all. What's next for The Tangler?"

"Well, Mary, we've got some exciting partnership deals coming up in the weeks ahead. I'm particularly pleased to announce that our entertainment news channel will soon be joined by the world's first predictive shopping channel: Good Deals Tomorrow."

"I understand there was some controversy recently, when you announced that you planned to introduce a predictive subscription service called 'Good Luck Tomorrow.' What was that all about?"

"Good Luck Tomorrow is our subscription service that helps our subscribers take advantage of the lottery system. But, most of the big lotteries are run by various government entities and, well, I predict they won't allow me to give people a better chance at winning. I foresee an injunction and a cease-and-desist order that I won't be able to say much more about after tomorrow."

"Wow. Well, there you have it, folks—a new prediction from The Tangler."

The animated Mary Wells Show logo swirled onto the screen. "We'll be right back with Mary Wells and our special guest Ty Thom," said the segment announcer, "right after these messages from our sponsors here on the Mary Wells Show."

"Welcome back. We're here with Ty Thom. Let's talk a little more about the service you call Good Luck Tomorrow. Ty, surely you must have considered the possibility that the government wouldn't allow you or anyone else to interfere with the huge money-making machine that is the government lottery system. Is this announcement of a subscription service that claims to provide advance notification of the winning number of a lottery just a publicity stunt?"

"Great question. No, it might sound like a publicity stunt, but I believe I really can provide my subscribers with early access to winning lottery numbers. I was also provided with legal advice suggesting that there is absolutely no law or statute in the books that specifically disallows such an action. So, until I hear otherwise, I encourage anyone who wants to have their share of winnings to subscribe to my service."

"All right. That's a pretty strong claim. What assurances do you provide your subscribers that you can in fact, deliver those winning numbers?"

"Mary, all one needs to do is to look at the fact that the Good News Tomorrow show has consistently delivered unassailably accurate information time and time again. I believe we're coming on 100 consecutive accurate predictions. I think those numbers speak for themselves. Officially, if you're a subscriber to the Good Luck Tomorrow service, you agree to the terms and conditions, which state that lotteries are considered a game of chance. I'm just sharing my gift and increasing their luck quotient."

"You speak about 'your gift.' It's a rather extraordinary claim."

"It is. And it's quite a responsibility. My mandate is to bring good news from tomorrow to the world of today. I believe—and it's clear that viewers agree—that the world can always benefit from a little more good news. I think that's the secret of the show's success. People know what to expect. And they know it's going to be good."

"I'm sure our viewers all want to know: how exactly is it that you are able to see the future like this?"

"Ah, yes, that's the secret, isn't it? That's why the show's got my name on it."

"You can't be more specific than that?"

"I'm just very lucky."

* * *

The next day, just as The Tangler had predicted, a cease-and-desist injunction was filed against him. Seven days later, he predicted the courts would overturn that decision on the grounds that there were no false claims being made nor laws being broken. Again, he was proven correct the very next day. At this point, everyone was talking about The Tangler. Stories and theories about him were everywhere.

Some speculated that his name was a clue: he was somehow entangling quantum particles—some of the armchair physicists claimed they were more correctly referred to as wave functions—in a way that allowed him to trace a path to a very specific outcome. Indeed, in one of his early interviews, he had specifically mentioned 'targeting a timeline I wish to be a part of.'"

As always, The Tangler's predictions were delivered by the silhouetted figure—a talking head on that signature blue background.

Genies are real, Ty Thom insisted. "But," he said, "I make the wishes and there's a completely scientific reason why—and when—my wishes come true. These genies are not magical servants or wish-granting slaves, as they are depicted in ancient Arabian fairy tales and children's stories. I make it my practice to make wishes come true."

"Ohh," smirked Mary Wells, the show host, "It sounds exciting when you put it like that."

There were a few titters from the audience, but not the response she'd hoped for.

The silhouetted figure shrugged. "Well, uh, it is. And when I reach that event horizon, the universe chooses the path that I am already a part of. The game is to tangle with the right opponents, and become entangled with paths that aren't dead-ends. I have to make sure the wish I'm making really can come true."

"So wishes can come true?"

"Absolutely, in a very real way. The quantum wave functions act as intradimensional travelers with a very specific role: to link together the quantum 'frames' that make up the multiverse. They do this via a method known as threading, which stitches the frames together into the tapestry of reality. Due to the multidimensional nature of reality, a certain amount of complexity is required in the connections between major events. The entanglement process I use manages the paths of threads through interstitial events to connect 'wishes' to choices. No matter how complex these interstitial events become, they will always connect. There's a little more to it, but it's all explained in my books."

"You mentioned the term *intradimensional*. Can you talk a little more about that?"

"Well the prefix intra, of course, means 'within' or 'inside.' So, the manifestation process I'm talking about is operating entirely within the standard dimensional framework—the here and now. There's no time-traveling, no do-overs. It's like a fully-manifested version of the old positive-thinking saying: You have to visualize success. I have reason to believe that it might also be possible to do exactly what I'm talking about entirely through the power of positive thinking."

"I think it's conceptually very much like the Japanese principle of Kaizen—small steps lead down the path toward improvement. In fact, my method uses a process very much like a Gemba board to walk through issues and potential countermeasures to calculate the optimal path to the desired outcome. The trick is to stay on that path, which often seems at odds with what one might consider better judgment. It's helped me become more trusting, I can tell you!"

Mary turned to the secondary camera. "We're be back with more advice from the man some call the world's luckiest guy right after this commercial break."

During the break, Mary held her hand over her left ear as she listened to her producer rant. "Get him off the physics stuff ASAP," he insisted. "It's a ratings killer. Steer him towards those sales numbers we talked about."

She turned to face the primary cam as the yellow light came on.

"Okay, we're back in ten."

She leaned toward Ty Thom. "We're back in five seconds. Okay?"

He smiled. The cameraman gave hand signals. Three ... two ...

"Welcome back. We're here with best-selling author, philanthropist, and influencer, Ty Thom."

"Ty, your biography lists so many remarkable titles and

achievements, it's absolutely mind-boggling. Your latest book, *The Last Tangle*, has enjoyed a position on *The New York Times* bestseller list for an unprecedented 240 weeks.

"Some are saying, however, that you manipulated that list to achieve this result by purchasing over 11,000 copies of the book yourself or through agents associated with yourself. How do you respond to that?"

"Well, Mary, it's a well-known fact that *The NYT* has never disclosed the proprietary algorithm that it uses to calculate its 'bestsellers' list; it's also true that the courts have already established that *The New York Times* is completely within its rights to exclude any book from its lists for any reason, including allegations of market manipulation. Moreover, it has also been established that simply getting onto that bestsellers list drives further book sales. The fact that my book is still on that list and doing very well at this time would seemingly refute your claims. I suggest to you that there are a great many people out there—including members of your own audience, I'm sure—who are interested in learning how to be more successful in a world that often seems to be designed to keep success in the hands of the few and opportunity out the reach of the many.

"It is, however, true that, in today's media environment, controversy drives the conversations, which in turn drive engagement. One of the key messages in my book is that you have to be brave. You have to be courageous enough to stay on the path to success no matter where it takes you. That's not always easy, but it is the way. I'm afraid I can't put it much more simply than that.

"Historically, these events have been interpreted by the superstitious as 'wishes fulfilled' and 'answers to prayers.' And, paradoxically, wishing, praying and other forms of positive thinking do, as I mentioned earlier, play a role in the outcomes of these events, although the principles at play are entirely scientific in nature. In all cases, the results that one may regard as good or bad luck is in fact a byproduct of the same types of quantum connections that the Tangler produces. But arbitrary notions of good and bad have nothing to do with these events. Rather, the effects are manifested through the same set of quantum field effects that have made the study of human consciousness such an ineffable and protracted mystery for the past five thousand years. But finally, the Tangler has opened that mystery box and revealed its contents to be discoverable by means of careful scientific study and the application of modern quantum dynamics theories. The resulting entanglement of the quantum strings allows those actions and choices to become what I call an engaged event that fulfills the requirement for coherence and complexity in that it does not collapse the wave function that, you might say, would otherwise have killed Schrödinger's cat."

"Well, I can't say I understood most of that, but some of our viewers are, I'm sure, familiar with Schrödinger's famous thought experiment."

"I strongly doubt that," grumbled the voice in her ear. "Two minutes to wrap."

"In your book, you mention Genies, Jinn, and Djinn. Can you tell us a little more about these characterizations—and what the differences between them are?"

"I'd be happy to but, again, these terms are really just a way of describing various classes of event handlers. The physical manifestations of the quantum connection types I describe in my books can be one or more of these event handlers, or they can be male or female humanoids, animals, or even trees, crystals, stones, liquids or some other manifestation. This leads to the very real possibility that legends of wishing stones, enchanted forests, powerful magic crystals, magic lamps, and so on, may have a basis in fact. In each case, the event handler acts as an operator on the quantum wave function, preventing its collapse that would otherwise destroy to connection to those intradimensional pathways. In this way, we minimize entropy and maximize coherence..."

"I'll have to stop you there," she interjected. "We're all out of time. It's a lot to take in. Well, that's our show for today. We've been talking with bestselling author, philanthropist, and influencer Ty Thom. I thank you for dropping by, Mr. Thom."

"It's been my pleasure."

* * *

Did you know?
A total eclipse of the sun occurs on Wednesday 13 August, 2436 UT, with maximum eclipse at 09:09 CST (01:09 UT). Hong Kong

* * *

19

Reconstruction

" The deeper we seek, the more is our wonder excited, the more is the dazzlement of our gaze.

—ABDUS SALAM

The next morning at 7:45 a.m., the telephone in George and Surya's hotel room rang. A woman's voice he didn't recognize asked to speak to George.

"This is George," he said. "To whom am I speaking?"

"I'm calling on behalf of Mister Thom," the woman said. "Regarding today's meetings, Mister Thom has requested that you attend the technical sessions between 9 a.m. and 3 p.m. alone. We will provide a driver for Miss Surya to go shopping or see the sights as she wishes, and we will have her back at the hotel by 3 p.m. Breakfast for you both will be provided in the Western restaurant on the first floor of the annex building. George, could you come down to the conference room C1 right now, please? Dr. Fidor has some technical information for you to review."

"I'll be there in a couple of minutes."

George put the phone down and quickly shaved with his electric razor. He gave Surya a quick kiss as he pulled on his jacket and headed out the door. "Have fun shopping. I'll see you this afternoon at three o'clock."

A moment later the phone rang again. Surya picked up the phone.

"Surya," said a deep voice. "Your identity has been compromised and we have to get you out of there right away. The driver of the blue limousine right out front will assist you and get you to safety. Do not tell anyone where you are going, and be sure you are not followed. Do you have a cell phone?"

"Yes, but I—"

"Turn it on and leave it in the hotel room safe," the voice said, interrupting her. "Then come down to the main entrance immediately and we'll handle the extraction from there via the blue limousine. Good luck."

"Darn it," replied Surya. "I was hoping to visit the temple later."

Click. The caller hung up.

Surya locked the phone in the hotel safe, then slid into her shoes and grabbed her purse. When she stepped into the elevator of the fifth floor, a man in a dark blue business suit was waiting inside. He punched the button for the fourth floor and handed her a magnetic bug.

"Attach this under the front seat," he said. "We'll be right behind you, listening in," he said. "If you're in trouble, make some noise." He got off at the fourth floor.

Surya straightened her hair in the elevator on the way down to the main floor.

The front doors opened and there was the blue limousine. A Caucasian woman held the door of the limo. "Coast is clear," she said quietly as Surya approached. "Nothing to worry about." She handed Surya a mobile phone. "Keep this phone with you and wait for further instructions."

Surya slid into the back seat. The driver looked in the rearview mirror and saw the worried look on Surya's face as the car pulled away from the hotel.

* * *

Dr. Fidor was waiting in Conference room C1 when George got there. "Thanks for coming down before breakfast. I wanted to be sure you had time to look these documents over before our meeting today." He handed George a leather folder. "I was hoping we could get started about nine o'clock. Will that work for you?"

"George nodded. He opened the folder and browsed through the diagrams, photos, and technical notes inside. "These diagrams are very impressive," he said. "Where did you get them?"

"I drew them, actually. So, thank you for the kind words about my drafting skills. I'm sure there are probably some faults to be found in there." Fidor unfolded a large blueprint.

"That's the most recent design," noted George. He didn't

mention it, but it was a nearly exact copy of the machine he had installed at Seahaven.

"I'm sure you recognize the design as the one commissioned by Nolan Stern."

"Yes, but I don't understand how you came to acquire it? The machine we built at Seahaven was lost during the big storm in 2435. The whole platform went down, with the machine on it."

"I would be doing you a great disservice if I didn't tell you the whole story about that. You see, I was hired by Nolan Stern to document the machine in as much detail as possible, in order to protect his rather significant investment. So, beginning in early 2432—April, I think was—I made several trips out there, during which I made detailed notes and copies of all of the work that you were doing to build the machine. I made backups of the firmware and software, the circuit diagrams, the design of the coils, the emitters, and so on—for safe keeping." Fidor fidgeted nervously. "I hope you understand," he added hastily, "there was never any intent to misuse those backups."

But you *did* misuse them! George's inner voice screamed. But he did his best to appear calm as he sought to find out exactly what Fidor had done.

"Have you shared this information with anyone else?" George asked. He could feel his ears burning,

"Oh, heavens, no," Fidor assured him. "I was the only one with access to those records. We realized fairly early on that an old oil rig out there in the middle of the ocean was not an ideal location to operate highly sensitive technical equipment without a backup. It was a defensive measure—and, if you don't mind me saying, such an abundance of caution proved to be warranted."

George did mind. Fidor had made a deal with this Mr. Thom based on a pilfered copy of *his* intellectual property. The arrogance of thinking that such an act was defensible in any way! But George managed to maintain a calm façade.

"I'll say," he said. "I was there when the rig collapsed and, believe me, it happened alarmingly quickly."

"Thank heavens you made it away safely," said Fidor. "I did my best to build an accurate copy of the machine, but of course, your design is... well, it's a work of genius. We're so fortunate to have you here to help us get it working again."

Dr. Fidor described his excitement of his first successful test of the copied machine. "It was a lifelong dream come true. And after literally thousands of hours of calibration, when we finally got the machine working, well, I can tell you, it was the thrill of a lifetime. It's a wonderful design."

"Thank you for the kind words, but—I must say—I'm disappointed that you've taken my design and sold a copy of it to this Mister Thom. I'm sure you can understand why that makes me angry."

"Of course," replied Fidor. "But really, it's not like that. If you'll grant me a few hours of your patience until we speak to Mr. Thom, I'm sure he will explain everything."

George was puzzled by Fidor's response, but he gave Fidor the benefit of the doubt. No sense in spoiling his chance to finally meet this Thom guy face to face. "By the way, am I ever going to meet this guy?"

"Yes. Mister Thom will be overseeing the sessions today and we expect he will have some questions and a full explanation for you later this afternoon."

"Good. I'm looking forward to that."

* * *

The ops team stationed in room 605, directly above George and Surya's room, recorded the phone conversations taking place in the suite below.

"...Mister Thom has requested that you attend the technical sessions before 3 p.m. alone."

"They might suspect something," surmised the director. "They're splitting them up."

The monitoring agent held up his hand. "Wait—phone's ringing again...."

The agent listened intently to the conversation between the unknown man and Surya. "...We have to get you out of there right away."

"Can you identify the caller's voice?" asked the director.

"I think it might be Thom's assistant," guessed the monitoring agent. He continued to listen. "Uh-oh. They're pretending to be us. Byrne is being instructed to get into a blue limousine via the front lobby."

"Tell Tan to intercept and intervene as soon as possible," said the director.

"I wonder if she thinks the instructions are coming from a trusted source," mused the agent.

"Doubtful," said the director, "but even if she's not sure, she'll be able to figure it out for certain as soon as she tests them with the pass phrase. It's unlikely they are going to be able to successfully respond to that."

"Has she dropped the phrase into the conversation yet?"

"I don't know. I missed a lot of that."

The director sighed. "Let's roll it back."

"I was hoping to visit the temple later." Surya said, awaiting the correct response to the pass phrase.

"Oh, wait—she just dropped it. And ... they hung up."

"That's good. She'll know what to do."

* * *

The blue limousine rolled along through the wide streets north of the Temple of the Sun. Surya looked out the window as they passed by an English-language sign outside a huge pair of stone gate-posts at the entrance of a place called Culture and Leisure Street. As the car rolled by, she caught tantalizing glimpses of the statues, fountains, and ornate roofs of the ancient buildings within.

The car had just turned northeast when the phone she had been given rang.

"You got to the limousine safely?" said a man's voice on the phone.

"Yes."

"Are you able to speak freely?"

"I think so." She didn't dare say anything more explicit in case the driver heard her.

"That's fine. Glad you're safe. Do you think you're being followed?"

Surya looked out the rear window as they passed a large

hotel. The whole area looked quite affluent. "No, I don't think so."

* * *

In the car behind, Tan saw Surya turn and look out the back window. "She's talking to someone on the phone."

"Yes, we can hear her. They are asking her about whether Gunderson is working for a foreign power."

"Is he?"

"Just a minute—they say they're taking her to the airport."

"Could be headed for Thom's home base."

"Seems doubtful. We think he's at the hotel with the rest of them."

"You're probably right. The car's now in the lane for international departures."

"Follow them and find out which flight they're trying to put her on. If possible, keep her off the plane and retrieve her. If that's not possible, and she seems to be safe, let her go and return to the hotel. We've got to get more eyes on Thom. He still hasn't shown."

"Will do."

"Good luck."

* * *

"Listen," the man on the phone said to Surya, "we've received some troubling reports about Mr. Gunderson. Do you think he's on the level? The people he's meeting with apparently are concerned that he might be working for a foreign power. Do you think that's the case?"

Surya could hardly believe her ears. She resisted the urge to give a voice to her incredulity. But it was as if a huge exclamation mark loomed before her. Apparently, Thom knew—or at least suspected—that she was an operative, and his people were fishing to find out if George was, too. For the first time, she considered the possibility that he might be. Was he the risk she should be worrying about? "Mmh—I don't think so," she said as the car pulled into the loading zone on the departures level.

"We're not going to chance it. We're evacuating you back to the United States. Your driver will help you get your ticket and get safely onto a plane. We'll arrange to have your luggage from the hotel sent back as well. Don't speak to or interact with anyone else prior to getting on the plane. We want to make sure you get back here safely. Take care."

Click.

Surya realized that maybe that's what this whole charade was about. They probably didn't know that she was aware of their attempt to trick her—or that it had been unsuccessful. That was intentional and she could play along with that. But maybe the question about George was the real gambit. They were worried that George was the real threat.

Surya had known something was wrong ever since the query phrase wasn't met with the correct response phrase. Now she needed to convince them that she was just a frightened little rabbit who had gotten into the limousine.

As she reviewed the sequence of events in her thoughts, she realized that the office might think she had blown her cover or compromised the mission. A compromised agent was always a liability. She needed to let them know what was going on. And she needed to get back to that hotel, or she would permanently damage the trust she'd spent years building with George.

The best options, it seemed, were to either get lost in the crowd at the airport or, failing that, somehow not get on the plane. If the driver was also planning to accompany her on the plane trip, both of those options might prove impossible to work around. She needed a third option—at least one that didn't require two back-to-back 17-hour plane trips.

If she could find a few minutes of private time, she could get a message to Emmett, her regular liaison at the office. But she didn't dare use the emergency beacon hidden in her purse while in the car. There was a rule against using high-risk communication channels to call the office, and even pay phones were on that list in China.

She watched as the driver left the vehicle and talked briefly with the traffic manager at the loading zone booth. The driver returned to the limo and opened her door. "Please follow me. Let's get you checked in properly."

"Here is a credit card for food and transportation and anything else you may require. Please give me that phone we supplied before getting on the airplane. We will contact you again via the usual channels."

* * *

The driver pulled the limo over in front of the international departures area, then opened the rear passenger door. She handed Surya a small carry-on bag. "This bag has some things you might need on your flight. And here in the side pocket is your first-class ticket back to Houston, Texas. Be careful not to lose that. It's a busy terminal. Follow me please."

Surya surreptitiously unzipped the bag and inspected the contents as she followed the woman to the departure gate. A small transparent bag containing cosmetics products, snacks, a pair of fairly nice sunglasses, a small towel, and yet another credit card.

The driver accompanied Surya on the train to the security inspection area. "You're not coming along on the flight, are you?"

"No, but my job is to get you safely on the plane, so I have a ticket so that I can accompany you through to the departure gate. Beyond that point, there are assistants that speak English at the desk if you have any questions. Stay in sight of the officers and I'm sure you'll be all right. Your flight leaves in about 45 minutes. The pre-boarding security check should take no more than 30 minutes. They will start boarding first-class passengers before everyone else, so be ready for that. Give me that burner phone and I'll dispose of it for you."

Surya hesitated for a moment.

"—Or, if you prefer, go ahead and smash it yourself."

Surya handed her the phone.

"I'll stand by at the departure gate to make sure you are able to board the plane safely," she said. "Nothing to worry about. Have a good flight."

* * *

46 minutes later

The phone on the desk next to the monitor displaying the video feed from the conference room buzzed once before being picked up. "It's Chaissie. The package has been delivered. No trouble."

Behind a plate-glass window at the airport, Chaissie watched as the plane climbed into the sky.

"That's good news," said the man's voice on the phone. "We'll see you back here soon."

* * *

"I'm a little worried about Surya," George said. "I haven't heard from her all day."

"Are her things still in the hotel room?"

"Yes."

"I'm sure she's just out shopping or enjoying the local museums and attractions. This is a very safe area, especially if she went with our limo driver. She'll take good care of Surya. She's probably using that credit card at the mall."

"You're probably right."

* * *

"Do you think the errors we are experiencing are not the fault of the machine, but are being caused by external interference?"

"Yes, I do. We're at a period in the solar cycle known as the solar maximum, and this particular cycle has been unusually disruptive, due to extensive sunspot activity. There have been a few X-class solar flares that certainly could damage sensitive electronic equipment, however, that doesn't appear to be the case here. I think what we're seeing in your jump logs are evidence of disruptions to the electrical grid—possibly exacerbated by transient errors resulting from sunspot activity. With that said, you've really done a good job calibrating the system. It's remarkably close to optimal. I'm impressed."

"So, what can we do? Could we build a Faraday cage or something like that to block the radiation?"

"You could, but it would have to be very large. We did some tests when we were developing the Bubblecraft and Starjumper technologies and we found that even a Faraday shield four times the size of the toroidal field we were trying to protect still interfered with the field effect. The field strength, as I'm sure you know, follows Coulomb's law."

"Yes," said Fidor, "the force is inversely proportional to the distance squared."

"I can tell you that a cage diameter of five times the size of the field will result in interference levels falling to one twenty-fifth of the initial value, so the resulting radiation levels should be minimal at anything beyond that. Unfortunately, for our portable designs, we didn't pursue the study of extremely large cage diameters, as that was outside the scope of our project requirements. In other words, you'll have to do some testing if you go down that path, but I do think there's a good chance of success at F/25 or greater."

"Well, that's not as quick a fix as Mister Thom was hoping for, but it sounds as though we might be able to develop a working solution without too much difficulty."

* * *

"Where have you been?" asked George when Surya, wearing a dark wig and looking somewhat worse for the wear, knocked on the hotel room door. "And what did you do with your room key?"

She flopped onto the bed. "Long story. I'm bushed."

"It can't be that long a story," George argued. "Where were you? I was worried about you."

"I hid in the Passenger Boarding Bridge and waited until the flight left. No big deal. I told them I fell asleep."

She pulled off the wig and kicked off her shoes. "I'm telling you George, this Mister Thom guy, and Fidor, and Miss whatever-her-name-is, these people can't be trusted. They deliberately lied to me and tried to get me to say that you were some sort of international criminal."

"Well, my background *does* look a bit sketchy to folks in certain circles. But these folks pay extremely well, and they need my help, so we're working together. Fortunately, they illegally reverse-engineered the jumpstation technology all on their own, so I'm kind of off the hook for that one."

"Well, just be careful. These people cannot be trusted."

"Say, why was your phone locked in the safe?"

"That's what I'm talking about."

* * *

"I need to speak to Emmett. It's Surya."

"This is Emmett. How's it going?"

"Ugh, the last 24 hours have not gone smoothly."

"Are you still in Beijing? Last we heard, you were on your way to the airport."

"Yeah, don't rub it in."

"Have you got anything on George, or are we wasting our time with him?"

"I was going to ask you the same question. I put the bug in the lapel pocket of his jacket as directed. Did it pick up anything?"

"Yeah, it was working today. We listened to a lot of technical mumbo-jumbo."

"That's George."

"We did hear him say that he had sold something to Nolan Stern. That's apparently how Fidor got hold of the design. He copied it from Stern. The comments were fairly vague, though. I don't think we could build much of a case, if that's all we've got."

"Unfortunately, there's no opportunity for me to personally attend those meetings at this point. They think I'm on a plane back to Houston."

"So, what's the point of being there? What's the best-case scenario?"

"Several possibilities: I think I can trust George not to disclose the fact that I'm still in Beijing. They don't know that I'm still in the picture—and it's always better to be invisible. I've got the disguise, so I'm able to move around freely now. I can be sure that we have ears wherever the meetings are being held. And sooner or later, Mister Thom is going to show up, so there's that."

"I don't like it. It's not enough to offset the risk. If you are identified, they'll abandon George, too. And besides, they're almost certainly watching George's movements, so the risk of you being seen or heard is high. It's no good."

"Oh, one more thing: Mister Thom's people gave me a cell phone and a couple of credit cards."

"Hm. Any interesting names in the contact list?"

"The only number in the phone book is labeled as 'call for help.' The driver of the limo implied that this was the number to reach her."

"Her? I thought the driver was a guy named Viktor."

"He *was* the driver when we first arrived in Beijing. But I think they wanted to be sure I wouldn't sneak away to the ladies' room and try to contact you, so they assigned a woman to keep an eye on me."

"I don't think they know anything about us. I think they were just fishing. An educated guess. Same goes for that question about George. It looks to me like Mister Thom is just being extra careful."

"I want you to turn off that that phone and then courier it and those two credit cards to the drop point and we'll investigate them. We'll set up a pattern of use in Houston to make it look like you're here. That will give you additional cover. At this point, we need two things from you: proof that George is selling U.S. military secrets, and details as to the identity of Mister Thom and what he is up to."

* * *

20

Restoration

Chaissie stepped onto the jump platform and climbed into the mini-pod. "I kind of like these smaller transit pods, she said. "I feel less claustrophobic with the glass panels."

"For these one-day jumps, there's much less risk of jumping into a catastrophe, so yes, it's nice to be able to choose comfort and still have some security," noted Dr. Emil Fidor.

"If you go on a big adventure to some time far in the future, we'll put you in the big one, for extra safety," he said.

"Only if you come with me, Emil," she said.

"Forty years ago, I'd have you taken you up on that offer, my dear. Alas, I've too much to do now. Are you ready? Let's do a final test of the Qmunicator."

She nodded and pressed the sync button. "Testing."

"I got it. Speech-to-text is working as expected."

"That's even better than usual," said Chaissie with a grin.

"Okay, here we go...."

Emil double-checked the jump vector and ran the program. As the initialization sequence counted down, he gave a thumbs-up to Chaissie. "See you in 24 hours."

Bzzt. The buzzer was followed by a flashing error light on the console. "What's wrong?" asked Chaissie.

"Hm. Just a minute. I'm pulling up the diagnostics," said Emil.

"It's that rotten checksum error again," he said. "Mr. Gunderson thinks it's the solar radiation. He believes it is more of a problem than the government is letting on. No sense in panicking people, you know?"

"If this thing's broken, it's really going to mess up the show."

Emil shook his head. "No flaws were found in the equipment; it all checked out okay. But the space weather is crazy right now. There has been a whole cluster of X45-class solar flares, and those are highly disruptive—among the most powerful ever recorded. It just means that we will have to get to work on that big Faraday cage that Mr. Gunderson recommended sooner rather than later. And not a bad idea to put off your suntanning for a little while until things calm down a bit. Until then, we will use a little more electricity and try again until we succeed. Here we go. Take two."

The initialization sequence counted down again. "Fingers crossed," said Emil.

Blink.

A split-second later, Chaissie was gone. Her expected time of arrival appeared on the screen and immediately began counting down. "Status looks good," said Emil to no one in particular. He imagined her in her usual routine, perusing the news feeds, looking for items that resembled good news. It usually took her three or four hours to compile a collection of 'good news' story candidates, which Mister Thom then whittled down for his show. She had never needed the full six hours, but it was a convenient way to avoid the time-travel equivalent of jetlag. They'd send her forward eighteen hours; she'd spend a few hours learning about what was going to happen tomorrow, and then jump back, where they'd finalize the editorial content from tomorrow for the show. Rinse and repeat.

Things would undoubtedly get more complicated—and probably a lot more profitable—with the launch of the new *Good Luck Tomorrow* and *Good Deals Tomorrow* subscriptions. Hopefully her seniority and editorial experience would count for something.

It struck Emil as ironic that she spent so much time worrying about her own future.

Just before the countdown completed, Emil and the

technicians returned to the jump platform to finish up the post-jump reporting and check that the transit pods were ready for reuse. Chaissie was far from the worst offender in keeping the transit pods clean, but they had to be checked. Right on time, the pod reappeared as the countdown reached the eighteenth hour.

The automated status report scrolled onto the control panel screen with its green header signifying successful completion.

The first thing Chaissie saw was Dr. Fidor's kind smile. He was always glad to see her return. "Hello! So glad to see you right on schedule. Well, that wasn't too bad, eh? No errors at all on that cycle."

Among the stories Chaissie presented at the editorial meeting later that afternoon was one called "The End of a Perfect Day" that detailed a ritual practice that had gained infamy for being banned at China's largest manufacturing facility, known as Megafactory City. This, of course, made it newsworthy, and its newsworthiness made it popular with the kids. "It's a wonderful good news headline," enthused Mister Thom. Chaissie tried to explain that the 'Perfect Day' ritual was controversial, but his mind was made up. "No one except the factory workers will know what it really means," insisted the silhouetted figure, "and when it comes true, it will add a whole new level of depth to our coverage of tomorrow's news. It will generate the kind of positive controversy we need to grow the platform."

"I have fantastic news," said Mister Thom when Chaissie and Dr. Fidor joined the meeting. "Not only have we been very fortunate to have our machine troubles addressed by possibly the world's foremost expert on these types of things, but I have some fantastic news to share about our new 'Good Luck' and 'Good Deals' programs. The editorial and features coordinator for these new properties will be..."

Chaissie couldn't forget how she felt when she heard the name that followed. It was as if her hopes turned suddenly to ash and were blown away on a stinging wind when fresh-faced 22-year-old Jasmine Jones, straight out of school with a marketing degree and no real-world experience whatsoever, was announced as the new face of the 'Good Luck' and 'Good Deals' properties.

"Mister Thom," Chaissie said, "I'm sorry, but I feel that I need to make a change in my career path. I'm resigning as your news gatherer effective immediately."

"Is this about Jasmine coming on board?"

"Well, *of course* it is," she felt like saying. She silently ran through the lines she had rehearsed but couldn't speak the words out loud. "Nobody likes to be blindsided, Mister Thom," she wanted to say. But then again, blindsiding people was pretty much Thom's whole business model. Instead, she shook her head and said "I would have preferred to have been advised of the plans to hire her prior to your public announcement."

She was a little surprised when she found herself saying: "I must also tell you that I have grave concerns over the way the situation with Ms. Byrne was handled. I really did not feel comfortable carrying out your requests. And lastly, I didn't feel that my concerns were taken seriously regarding the controversial nature of stories like 'A Perfect Day.'"

"I'm disappointed to hear about your plans to leave so suddenly," he said. "I need you to stay on for two weeks until I hire a replacement."

"I'm sorry, I cannot do that," she said firmly. "I have made other plans."

He pressed the matter further. "I insist that you do. It's common courtesy in business matters such as these," he argued.

She looked disdainfully at the figure, silhouetted as always on the video display. Suddenly, the words spilled out of her mouth. "Look, I've done everything you've asked ever since the Seahaven days, and I'm grateful that you pretty much saved my life when we had to leave in such a hurry, during that huge storm. I've played along with calling you Mister Thom, as you requested. But I really felt uncomfortable with tricking Surya Byrne into a car and onto an airplane under false pretenses. We were basically kidnapping her at that point, and that's absolutely unacceptable to me. Honestly, I think I have PTSD after everything that's happened. I'm a nervous wreck. And I'm getting cooked by that giant microwave oven of yours every time I jump, which is literally every day. I'm done. Goodbye Nolan."

21

Wake Up Call

"Hurry up—it's starting!"

The four workers sharing the small one-room apartment in the Megaconn dormitory area sat together on the sofa with their bowls of noodles. Good News Tomorrow was their favorite show and they loved to pronounce the sounds of the American English words spoken by the announcer: "And now, here he is, your host with the most Good News Tomorrow... Ty Thom, The Tangler!"

The live audience applauded enthusiastically.

The show's gimmick was that Ty was somehow able to make wishes and have them come true. And Ty only wished for good news. The fact that all the good news he wished for would miraculously come to pass the very next day was the hook that had made it the number one show in its time slot. Asian and English-speaking audiences alike just couldn't get enough of *Good News Tomorrow*.

The success of the show had made Ty Thom a major

celebrity, too. Investigative reporters discovered that Thom's real name was Nolan Stern. Interestingly, they noted, Nolan Stern's birth father had been a *bona fide* seer, too. He had verifiably made more than 100 predictions, all of which had come true. It looked like the 'seer gene' had been passed on.

* * *

The suicide rate was up in Megafactory City and Li Hai had been hired by the American client to find out why the production line was running behind schedule. Mr. Hai met with the floor supervisor, who assured him that everything was under control. Mr. Hai explained that he had been hired by the American client as a health and safety officer, tasked with investigating the Megaconn worker conditions. "Part of my role," he explained, "is to document the causes of the latest casualties and to help get the production numbers back up to the contractually required levels." Mr. Hai didn't mention it, but the other part of his role was to advise the client on whether Megaconn management was properly and effectively complying with those contractual requirements.

Mr. Hai studied the data on his tablet for a moment before speaking. "Your own investigation," he said emphatically, "reveals that a large number of workers in Megafactory City have been killing themselves—but why?"

The floor supervisor adjusted his glasses. "There are a few different reasons," he said. "Some workers don't get along well with the robotic line managers. Others don't respond well to the automated termination of employment that occurs when time-limit targets are exceeded. And some simply don't like the type of work we're offering or the rate of pay."

Either the floor manager wasn't aware of it, or declined to mention it, but there was another big reason: something of a suicide cult had sprung up among the workers. It started as a challenge, then became a meme. By taking the challenge, it was claimed, one could finally break free of the soul-killing cycle of work-eat-sleep by playing a little game.

They called it "Wake Up Call" and dared each other to play the game with all its dangerous consequences.

At first, of course, it was all but impossible to find any-one willing to admit they had even heard of such a game, but Mr. Hai continued his interviews and investigations until he had a group of witnesses willing and able to corroborate descriptions of how the deadly game was played.

One of the interviewed workers hold him she had been present during the final hours of one game-player and had witnessed him participating in a highly stylized ritual before throwing himself into the biofuel bin, where his life's work became little more than a tragic statistic.

* * *

"It works like this," she said. "Every morning at 6:00 a.m., all Megafactory workers get an automated wake-up call from Smart Work Central. When the call comes in, it delivers a daily motivational message, such as 'We work smarter, so you don't have to' or 'Be smart—you can earn five percent more by working overtime today.' Or 'Only two days until pay-day. You're doing great!' Workers can cycle through a random playlist of the complete monthly cycle of these wake-up call inanities, and from this activity, a simple game emerged. Two or more workers each touch the 'Wake Up' buttons on their company-issued smartphones. If the platitudes are the same, they proceed to the 'Motivational Message Finals', until only one is left. As the playlist is very large, this game can take several days or even weeks to reach its conclusion. In some months, the month-end arrives before a winner is declared, and the cycle begins anew. If and when a 'winner' is declared, the runner-up becomes their 'majordomo' for a perfect day, in which both players call in sick and take the day off work. The majordomo's job is to make the winner feel as comfortable and lucky as possible."

"I see," said Mr. Hai. "Thank you. I may have more questions for you about this later."

"Please don't use my name or reveal my location in the workline," said the young woman. "I need this job."

"Your anonymity is assured," Mr. Hai promised her.

When the company found out that this game was going on, it attempted to co-opt the premise by announcing a 'Perfect Day' worker ten percent bonus, although those who accepted this gratuity were roundly shamed by their peers.

Another interviewee, a young woman who said her name was Shirlee, told Mr. Hai that there was more to the game than the first young woman had let on. Shirlee told him she had been a majordomo on several Perfect Days.

As they sat on a bench at the factory cafeteria, she apologized that she was not able to be interviewed at her home. She explained that she was without a permanent address after her relationship with a co-worker ended in his death.

"You have no home?"

"I live on an abandoned bus with three other people. Used to be four. The factory provides washrooms, showers and affordable food, so it's not a bad life—certainly better than being under a piece of cardboard in the park," she said.

"From the original game," she told him, "a darker variant has emerged, in which the Perfect Day ends with the winner —if they are brave enough, with the help of the majordomo, if they are willing enough—putting on what is known as The Exit Bag."

"What's that?" asked Li Hai.

"The Exit Bag is a bag that fits over the head, with an elastic to hold it tight around the neck. It fills with helium, which fools the body into thinking it's breathing oxygen. And, thanks to the helium, one's last words are captured by the majordomo at 'Day's End' in a darkly comic fashion— perfect for posting on social media. It's the ultimate end to one's Perfect Day, when the megacorporation's promise of 'Working for a More Prosperous Tomorrow' becomes simply unbearable—and the advertising revenues accrued from the millions of views of the deceased party's Day's End speech ends up providing a substantial revenue stream for the departed's bereaved family."

"But why are the Megaconn workers so depressed?" Mr. Hai asked her.

"It's because they know what's really going on in Megafactory City."

"And what exactly *is* going on?"

"Meet me at line number 9 here tomorrow at 8:05 a.m. and I will show you," she promised.

* * *

The next morning, Mr. Hai had traded in his blue business suit for a pair of Megaconn worker's coveralls and his Corinthian leather briefcase for a plastic access card holder. He walked from his assigned apartment in the Minzhi residential district and caught the 7 a.m. shuttle bus heading north along the Meiguan Expressway The shuttle bus stopped only twice on the way there: once at the Shenzhen entrance and once at the Megaconn Technology group of buildings. From there it proceeded to the drop-off point just inside the west gate of Megafactory City where Mr. Hai planned to begin his investigation.

There, tens of thousands of workers (a mere fraction of the 350,000 workers occupying the other workfloors of Megafactory City), all dressed in their gray-and-blue coveralls, streamed from what looked like a thousand other shuttle buses, all lined up in the huge drop-off lot, between the massive distribution center building and the canteen adjoining the main Megafactory complex.

After a disappointingly bland Guangdong-style Dim Sum breakfast and a cup of lukewarm morning tea, Mr. Hai followed the stream of workers to the card-swipe zone at the factory.

Once inside, he spotted the line numbers hanging from the beams. Rows one through three were robot docks. He walked briskly past the robots as they noisily stacked and packed on each of the dock lines. As usual, there was no line number four. In its place was a buffer zone marked with yellow painted stripes between the bot docks and the worklines. Ahead were the human workers, on lines that stretched nearly as far as the eye could see. And there, just ahead, was line number 9.

He looked at his watch. 8:04 a.m. At 8:05 CST, he was supposed to meet Shirlee here for what she had promised him would be more information.

At exactly 8:05, Shirlee stepped into the aisle underneath the sign for line nine. "We can't stay here," she whispered. "Just follow me and keep your head down."

They walked briskly past two rows of workers assembling EHAD headsets.

"The city's population just dropped below the 20 million mark for the first time in 50 years," she said. "That's still a lot of people, but it sure is an improvement from my grandfather's era."

"Of course, about a third of the population around here is robots now."

"At least!" said Shirlee.

She helped Mr. Hai get past the workdesk, where he saw first-hand the reality on the factory floor.

* * *

The Megaconn Jumpstation had opened in 2409 on the power of an intriguing offer. Make the jump and get a job, guaranteed. The only conditions were that you had to hold a Chinese work permit and you had to agree to work at the job for at least twelve months. It seemed like an attractive offer, especially when word spread online that the jumpstations in America were charging $180,000 U.S. dollars for a jump—but without the guarantee of job when you get there.

As soon as the announcement hit the news, lineups sprang up outside the Megaconn jumpstation building, days in advance of the official opening. Once the facility opened, the lineups increased, often resulting in people having to sleep in the line if they didn't manage to make it to the front of the line by closing time.

Part of the "Wake Up Call" challenge, she explained, is to record a "blink" video. It became popular for people to record their 'blink' experiences and post the often bizarrely disorienting 'blink videos' online.

One second, a group of six people would be standing in the autotram that served as the Megaconn equivalent of a transit pod. Then suddenly, the background would instantly change, as would the jumper's mood. The tram would then autonomously move the now-celebratory group off the platform and shuttle them next door to the factory worker orientation area, as another autotram pulled onto the pad, ready to load the next group.

Once their orientation session was complete, the arriving jumpers were moved onto the factory production line. You could always tell the newbies, as they were wearing the telltale augmented reality headsets that provided the training and assembly instructions they would soon know by heart as they worked assembling and packaging EHAD cerebral-enhancement modules.

* * *

Shirlee pointed to a set of windows in an area on the upper-level platform overlooking the factory floor. "Do you see that office and that row of cameras?"

Mr. Hai nodded.

"Another part of the challenge is to commit and record a violation without getting caught."

"That's where the Takers are. They monitor the workers and if there are any violations, they take them away."

"Where do they take them?"

"Out. They just take them out of the factory and put them on a tram. I'm not sure but I've heard that it goes back to the residential area. That might depend on the infraction, I don't know. But keep your eye on that room. There are usually a couple of take-outs each day."

* * *

Inside the Monitoring Station, three Takers studied their respective banks of monitors. The auto-detector flagged a worker on line 9 for not being at the appointed station.

Moments later, the auto-detector added a secondary log entry. "Worker at Line 9, Seat 4 appears to be taking unauthorized photos or videos. Critical intervention required."

As the video zoomed in on Seat 4, Mr. Hai continued to record the events. He described the events he was seeing in an impassive whisper. "Two bots have just emerged from the dock on line 2. They are coming this way. There's a yellow light flashing. People are clearing out of the way. They seem to know what's going on. It looks like they will be going straight past me. There's no obvious disturbance anywhere on this line that I can see. Wait. They are slowing down. Oh—"

The recorder clattered to the table as the bots grabbed the surprised Mr. Hai and pulled him away from the production line. Each bot held one of his arms and they rolled sideways, one after the other, with him in the middle as they carried him away toward the security desk at the front door.

When they got there, the bots released their grip on Mr. Hai's arms and he fell to the floor in front of the Security Desk manager.

The manager held out his hand. "Hand over your employee badge," he commanded.

"You have been found in violation of multiple ordinances and are hereby required to turn over any and all recordings and other evidence of factory practices and procedures."

Like hell, thought Li Hai.

"Failure to comply with factory rules may result in criminal prosecution or other punitive actions," the manager warned him.

"I'd like to have my recorder back now. Please." said Li Hai with a wholly insincere tone of politeness.

"This device is believed to contain company proprietary information and will be returned to you only after it is unlocked and inspected," the Security Manager said.

"All right, give it here; I'll unlock it."

"You will be required to delete all copies of any infringing materials recorded by any device in your possession," the manager warned him.

Yes, yes. I get it." He deleted the interview videos, the shots of the bots, and the other still photos he had captured. "There. Happy?"

The Security Manager inspected the phone and returned it to Li Hai. "Thank you for your compliance. Please use the door marked Exit to leave the building and exit the factory property promptly. Have a nice day."

As annoyed as he was to have the two bots follow him to the exit, Mr. Hai wasn't concerned about being forced to delete the videos; he had automatically uploaded everything to the cloud upon creation. He would make sure his client —and others who might have thought that the company adhered to regulations and treated its employees with at least a modicum of respect—saw what was really going on in MegaFactory City.

Mr. Hai was mildly alarmed when he returned home to find a strange vehicle parked on the street outside his home with two men in it. But that was nothing compared to the shock he experienced when he opened the front door of his apartment. His tiny apartment had been ransacked. It was a mess.

His anger gave way to worry that the intruders might also have attacked his online files. They hadn't—but when he signed in to his cloud account to check if the files were still there, they gained access to his biometric signature via a pass-key logger they had installed.

Li Hai compiled his evidence into an exposé video and narrated a voiceover track detailing the discoveries he had made of the human rights abuses occurring at the factory. He uploaded the video and sent the American client a link to the private file.

The next day, he awoke to find an angry email from the client, demanding to know why he had posted the video publicly.

He tried to explain that he hadn't, but ended up apologizing and promising to fix the issue.

When he checked the video, he got another shock. The video had been replaced and the voiceover track altered.

Images of smiling, happy workers were shown as the narrator spoke in glowing terms about the factory conditions.

"We are handling the crisis," the narrator said. "Our investigation has shown that, without a doubt, the fault clearly lies with the victims. These are societal problems and by rigorously enforcing the rules of a just society, we can work through them."

"We now require that employees sign a waiver stating that Megaconn will not be made liable if any individuals violate corporate policy."

* * *

That evening, on Good News Tomorrow, Ty Thom predicted an inspector at Megafactory City would learn what it was like to have a perfect day.

* * *

22

A Perfect Day

" The more he goes back, the further he will be able "
to see ahead.

—HENRY FORD

Exhausted, Li Hai fell asleep after spending all day cleaning up his ransacked apartment. In the middle of the night, a tremendously loud noise woke him up with a start as three masked figures burst into his room and grabbed him. They pulled a bag over his head and dragged him past the shattered front door, down the stairs and onto the street where he heard the sound of a minivan door sliding open. They pushed him inside and slammed the door shut.

After many twists and turns, the vehicle turned off the smooth road onto a gravel surface. The silent assailants pulled him out of the van and wrestled him up a short flight of stairs.

He heard the sound of a heavy door being unlocked and, a moment later, he was pushed onto an uncomfortable chair. He heard a man who sounded like he was in in the next room speaking in Mandarin say something about "this American lackey." As Li Hai shifted in his seat to listen more closely, a man speaking in English pressed him roughly back into the chair and told him to sit still and be quiet—or else.

He heard the sound of footsteps, followed by the door closing and a lock turning. And then it was silent.

Li Hai lifted the bag up and peered at his surroundings. In the small, drab room, there was a small metal table with a tablet on it, a gray metal door, and a light in the ceiling. No windows, no mirrors. The clock said 5:59.

The tablet's display changed to 6:00 and music began to play. "This is your wake-up call," the voice said in English. "We work smarter, so you don't have to."

Li Hai realized that the deadly game that had been played by the employees of Megaconn was now playing out with him as the unwilling participant.

"Welcome to your Perfect Day. You're a winner!" said the voice from the tablet. "You're doing great! I'll be your major-domo. My job is to make you feel as comfortable and lucky as possible."

* * *

The next morning, authorities responding to an anony-mous tip found Li Hai with an Exit Bag over his head and his termination of employment slip on the table beside him. It was, they concluded, death by asphyxiation—another deadly game of Wake-Up Call—that was to blame.

This theory was borne out later that day, when the search engines uncovered video clips of a woman identified as a known perpetrator of Wake-Up Call suicide assistance. The newly discovered clips showed her explaining the rules of the game to Mr. Hai, and her role as majordomo.

A subsequent search for the party identified by the automated video systems as Shirlee Zhang proved fruitless. Ms. Zhang was no longer at the address given on her employment record and the company decided not to turn the missing person report over to the authorities. The identity of the individual who filed the anonymous report about the fate of Mister Hai was never discovered.

The Megaconn HR Knowledge Graph identified Shirlee Zhang as the party most likely to have filed the report; she was also identified as a suspect or otherwise implicated in several other incidents involving now-deceased former employees, but the findings were inconclusive and her current whereabouts were never discovered. Shirlee never returned to the factory; her personal interests page was updated a few times after her last reported sighting; it now listed her as an ex-domo. The case was closed—another deadly game of Wake-Up Call had led to the end of a Perfect Day for Mister Hai.

* * *

Shirlee laid low during the weeks that followed. She had heard stories of domos being threatened, hunted, and even killed by members of an unknown underworld organization rumored to be linked to the industrial conglomerate that owned and operated the factories in Megafactory City. They controlled the businesses, but were also rumored to wield control over the policing of the area, as well.

Mr. Hai had sent her a link to both an early draft and the final investigation report; when she saw the final version, she could tell by the edits that something was wrong. The entire *tone* of it had changed dramatically. It went from being an investigative report to a corporate puff piece. She didn't know who was responsible for the edits, but she was sure it wasn't Mister Hai.

She asked the other three people who lived on the bus who they thought might be responsible and asked them for their opinions on what she should do.

They all agreed that it seemed most likely that his disappearance and death were direct results of the company finding out that they were being investigated. There were, after all, many millions of American dollars at stake here. They also expressed concerns that the Chinese government, too, might be in on some sort of massive cover-up. But Shirlee hadn't expected what would happen next. Upon hearing about Shirlee's situation, one of the other three bus-mates reacted by asking her to leave immediately... and the other two immediately voiced their support of his position.

"Why? I've done nothing wrong," Shirlee insisted.

The others argued that she was clearly a hunted person and had thus placed them all in jeopardy. They couldn't risk losing their jobs, and they couldn't afford to live elsewhere.

Shirlee begged for them to give her a week to find another place to stay; they insisted on a maximum of 48 hours.

They weren't wrong, either. The port authority police and airline security personnel had both been placed on high alert and told to watch for movement or attempts to emigrate by a Chinese citizen identified as Shirlee Zhang. It was only the fact that she was a person of no fixed address that thwarted their attempts to apprehend her.

* * *

"Hello?"

"Is this Li Yan Zhang, daughter of Sun Yat Zhang and Jenny Chen?"

"Yes ... who is this?"

"My name is Shirlee Zhang. I'm your cousin."

"Wow. What a ... *nice* surprise. Uh ... where are you?"

"I'm in China. In Beijing, actually."

"Your English is excellent."

"I worked for an American client. Listen, I don't want to take up too much of your time, but I'm in a bit of trouble. I know this probably sounds like a scam, but I swear, I'm only calling because I don't know anyone else I can trust. Look, I know this sounds weird, but people are trying to hunt me down and if they find me, they'll kill me."

"Oh my god. You should go to the police."

"I think they're the ones who are after me. I think others are after me too. My American friend just got killed yesterday and now they're after me. I'll give you anything you want if you can somehow help me get away from them. Please."

"Why are they after you? What did you do?"

"I just told the truth to an investigator about what I'd seen at the factory and now they people that own the factory are trying to shut me up—permanently. The investigator is the guy they killed yesterday. They broke his door down and took him away and they killed him. To protect their profits. I know it sounds unbelievable, but I swear it's true. They got him and now they're after me. I beg you—please, please help me."

Li Yan had to think for a moment to make sure she wasn't being scammed. "Uh, do you have any ID or any anything you can send me to prove you are who you say you are? What have you got?"

"I will send you pics of all the ID I have. I will also send you some other proof," Shirlee promised.

An hour later, a message from Shirlee arrived. In it were images of all her employment records, bank accounts, and passport records. *This is everything I have*, she wrote. *I hope it's enough for you to trust me. I am a little short on money to pay for a plane ticket to Washington, but I have enclosed my credentials for my bank account to prove my sincerity.*

Li Yan studied the identification and ran a few verifications. Everything checked out. She transferred a few dollars out of the bank account using the supplied credentials. It, too, checked out. No scammer would do that, she decided.

"All right," Li Yan wrote, "I will help you get to Washington. When do you want to make the trip?"

"Right away, please," Shirlee replied.

"I can get you on a ship heading to America and the ID you'll need to get into the country. How does that sound?"

"Wouldn't it be easier to travel by air? I'm not far from the Daxing International Airport."

"The security at the airports is pretty much impossible to get around. I can't get access to the kind of ID that can fool those airport scanners. It's too risky."

"I suppose. Too bad. The Daxing District is so close to where I live. Oh well, a ship then. What do you suggest?"

Li Yan couldn't tell Shirlee how she knew it was coming, but she had been waiting for this call for ten years. "I believe you," she assured Shirlee. "I've arranged for a passport under the same of Suni Zheng and all the ID you will need to be able to be able to board a ship that will be leaving from the Port of Tianjin at 4 o'clock this afternoon. The bus takes about three and a half hours to get to the port, so you should have plenty of time if you leave in the next couple of hours. You'll be going to board a ship named the Golden Ray at dock 14B. Show your ID to the boarding agent there. His name is Chi Weng. Can you do that?"

"Yes. Where will the boat be going?"

"It will arrive in Seattle, Washington. And I'll be waiting at the dock in Seattle when you arrive. Don't worry. Everything will be taken care of. Just remember: your name is Suni Zheng."

All she had to do now was to send the information back to herself.

* * *

23

The Infinity Machine

As she stood on the deck of the boat that night, Shirlee looked up at the aurora borealis undulating like a phosphorescent dragon across the northern sky.

With a crossing time of almost three weeks, Shirlee had plenty of time to think about what, if anything, she wanted to do in the wake of Li Hai's death.

A part of her wanted to expose Megaconn's culture of corporate corruption and force the company to face the consequences for the inhumane ways it had been treating its workers for so long. By publicly speaking out about what she had learned and seen firsthand, she could be an agent for change. Another part wanted to remain anonymous. If she ever had to return to China, it would be best not to be on enemy radar. And still another part vowed never to return. It had taken so long to get out—it would be foolish to squander this great opportunity.

By the time the west coast of North America was in sight,

she had become comfortable with the idea of anonymously exposing the corruption she had seen. That would be enough.

The beauty of the coastlines bordering the Salish sea was breathtaking, as the ship neared its Seattle port, the green hills on the islands in the Puget Sound seemed to go on forever. At last, the city and its harbor came into view and the ship reduced its engine speed for the final entry into port.

As promised, Li Yan was waiting outside the customs area when Shirlee got there. She was holding a sign that said Suni Zheng.

Shirlee waved excitedly when she saw the sign. "Cousin!" she shouted.

Li Yan looked relieved. "Oh, I can't tell you how relieved to see you here," she said with a smile.

"Me too!"

"Let's get out of here. I have a car out front."

The car's passenger-side falcon wing door lifted up as they approached. "Wow. Very fancy."

Hey, I hope you don't mind me asking, but ... when were you born?"

Li Yan laughed. "Heh. I don't tell anybody that information. I know why you're asking, though. Your parents died, what, ten years ago or so?"

"Yes, ten years this July."

"And did you look up when my parents died?"

"Yes. That's... that's why I was wondering... Did you go through the Infinity Machine?"

"I've never heard that term before. But I think I know what you're talking about."

"It's basically a time machine that instantly moves you as far forward in time as you want to go."

"Yeah, we have a device like that in the lab where I work that we call a Jump Station. It lets you jump forward in time. I've used it a few times. Quite a few times, actually."

"I knew it!" said Shirlee.

"So, you guys have one of those in China? Huh."

"Oh, more than one—lots. They use them as recruiting systems, you might say. People are promised a job if they go through the Infinity Machine. They just have to be eligible to work in China, and promise to work for at least twelve months."

"And you went through it?"

"Yes. I kind of crashed out of the 12-month commitment, though. I got into some trouble and lost my apartment, so I was more or less homeless for a while. And then I got into even more trouble, as I explained."

"Yeah, listen. You'll have to stay out of trouble here. I wouldn't want to see you get extradited back to China for something stupid. Just lay low and find a job using your new ID. You can stay with me until you get your own place. You'll be fine."

"I really cannot thank you enough."

"Just stay out of trouble. That's all I ask."

"By the way, are you married, or anything like that?" Shirlee asked.

Li Yan smiled. "No, although I do have kind of a steady boyfriend," she said. "His name is Karl."

"How long have you two been together?"

"Oh, you know, a few years." She didn't like to think about the actual number of years. The truth was, it had been 395 years since their first fling. Maybe six years of actual time together since then. That was the weird thing about jumping forward. It made the moments of real time in between the jumps seem more real, more vital. All the rest of it was just a forgotten dream.

She thought for a moment. "Hey, do you mind if I invite him over tomorrow night? I'm sure he'd like to meet you."

"Sure. That sounds great."

"Oh, there's one thing I have to warn you about. He's a bit sensitive about the color of his skin...."

"Oh, I'm totally cool with that. Is he brown or...?"

"He's blue, actually. Have you seen that gene hack that turns your skin blue?"

"No, I've never seen that."

"Well, you'll probably see it tomorrow. Just don't make a big deal about it. He doesn't really like to talk about it."

"I totally understand."

* * *

The next evening, just before six, Shirlee beamed as Li Yan pulled dresses, blouses, and skirts off their hangers and handed them to her to try on. Shirlee wasn't accustomed to having so many extravagant choices available; they all looked wonderful to her. Fortunately, she was about the same height and build as her older cousin, so the clothes fit her well.

The exercise was fun for Li Yan, too. She never had a little sister, so this was the first time in a long time she had the chance to share an experience like this with someone.

* * *

Karl had been searching for George for months, but he couldn't find him anywhere. He had grown increasingly frustrated and depressed as the weeks went by. He felt like he was losing his mind.

At the dinner table, Li Yan could see that things were worse than usual tonight. Karl was avoiding eye contact and was uncharacteristically terse when spoken to. When he went to the kitchen after dinner, she followed him and cornered him near the pantry. "What's going on?" she whispered. "Is it something about Shirlee?"

"Not at all," he insisted. "It's just, well, you know... I am worried that I'm not going to find George here. I just have to ... you know ... keep looking."

Exasperated, she poked at his chest. "No. You do *not* have to do that. You don't have to keep chasing this *apparition*. Why can't you choose the good life we have here?" He just stared at her, looking miserable and ashamed.

She growled in frustration. "And hear me now: I am not jumping again, period. If you jump, you will *lose* me, and I will *never* forgive you. I need you *here*. Shirlee needs you here."

"I know that and I am truly sorry. I just ... don't belong here."

"So, you're going to jump again, is that it? Goddammit. You need to stop being so *selfish*. Right now, Shirlee needs family and stability and I refuse to abandon her. I wish you could see how heartless you've become. Don't you care about me?"

"Li…" he mumbled. "I don't know why, but I just feel like I've lost everything. Everything."

"Maybe a mental health professional could help," she suggested.

"I dunno." He rubbed his face, as he often did when the panic started.

"Look, I understand how you are feeling and know that your friend is important to you."

"It's not just George," he interjected. "It's me."

"I know, baby, I do want to help, I really do. So come back to the table and let's help Shirlee tonight. We can talk about the rest of it tomorrow, hey? What do you say?"

"I've got to go for a walk," Karl insisted.

Maybe that would help. He was still out when she and Shirlee finished their tea. She bade Shirlee goodnight and stayed up for a while longer, hoping he'd return in a better mood. An hour later, she fell asleep on the couch.

* * *

She woke up the next morning and found Karl back in the bed. He stirred when she got out of the bed and managed to sound almost repentant when he apologized for being out so late. He gratefully accepted a cup of coffee and she didn't challenge him further on the previous evening's topics or activities. She had, of course, seen these sorts of moods before. This time, however, Li Yan realized that Shirlee needed her even more than Karl did. She found purpose and satisfaction in caring for Shirlee and felt uncharacteristically free of the burden of having to always be an anchor for Karl. She realized she was at last ready and willing to let Karl stand or fall on his own.

Li Yan didn't challenge him on his uncaring behavior again after that night, but Karl realized that something had shifted. He realized that that she needed someone who could be there for her and for Shirlee—and that he had some work to do to be there for them in a supportive role.

This feeling of having lost everything nagged at him. He thought of Miran. She had always been there for him when he needed her. He decided to reach out to her and ask for her help.

Miran was happy to hear from Karl. She knew that he had been struggling, and she wanted to help him. She invited him over to her house, and they spent the day together. They talked about everything that had happened, and Karl felt like he was finally starting to heal.

"Did you have any luck finding George?" Miran asked him.

"Maybe," Karl replied. "I put out queries that I figured would get picked up by his agents, as you suggested, and I did get a couple of responses. They are just automated replies, but I think they will get to him, if they haven't already."

"That's great. What's next?"

"Well, that fact that he's left bots here means he is either still in this time-frame, or he *was* here. I'll just let him know that I'm looking for him. I'm pretty sure he'll respond when he sees it's me."

"He doesn't owe you any money or anything like that, does he?"

"God no. I'd never find him if that were the case."

* * *

A few weeks later, Karl got a message from Li Yan.

Any word from George?

No, but I'm sure he is aware that I was looking for him. He must have his reasons for whatever he's doing, wrote Karl.

Do you want to come back home?

I do. I've got a new contract going with NASA. There might be some work here for you too. Interested?

Maybe—Let's talk about it when you get here.

See you soon.

* * *

Did you know?

Elumination makes it easy to change your life. Find love and live life to its fullest with Elumination, where everyone gets a second chance.

* * *

24

Perihelion

"When I was a young man, Dirac was my hero. He made a breakthrough, a new method of doing physics. He had the courage to simply guess at the form of an equation, the equation we now call the Dirac equation, and to try to interpret it afterwards."

—RICHARD FEYNMAN

Ever since that meeting with Fidor, an idea had been rattling around in George's brain. If electromagnetic interference is the problem, then a Faraday Cage is the answer. Back in the early days of testing, they had done some Faraday shield tests on the old V1 jumpstation design, but the geomagnetic sync signals that the HELX high energy large accelerator used to stabilize its toroidal fields and lock onto a fixed location on the earth were severely disrupted by the shield and they abandoned the idea.

Now, however, with the new onboard geosyncronous designs of the Bubblecraft and the space-based Starjumper field generators, it seemed to George that it was time to revisit the idea. After all, solar radiation was more of an issue than ever, and this was even more of an issue in space. If he could just get it working, NASA's ASTRA division would probably be an eager customer. And even if they weren't, Fidor and the mysterious Mister Thom definitely would.

George received Andrew's permission to hang onto the Bubblecraft for another twelve months and it became his primary test platform. He bought one of the old Andna trucks—at a bargain price—at auction and began fabricating a metal mesh cage on the inside of the cargo box of the truck.

Eventually, by carefully calibrating the field strength and precisely positioning the Bubblecraft inside the truck, the Faraday Cage produced its desired shielding effect. After pulling the Bubblecraft in and out of the truck innumerable times, he built a set of floor clamps to make it easier to lock the craft into the required position, as well. For George, convenience, not necessity, was the mother of invention.

* * *

"It's very frustrating," conceded Karl, as he worked with Li Yan on the ASTRA resonant impulses model. "I know it's possible, but I just can't seem to replicate the effect of that quantum resonance value that we used to sync to that ionospheric signal from 1947. It seems like it should be working, but it just doesn't. I wish I could study that quantum radar signal from '47. It seems like they didn't document it fully."

"Probably for reasons of national security," suggested Li Yan.

She speculated that it might be a past-directed CTC effect at work—perhaps a Kerr Metric or a time-orientable Lorentzian manifold with a closed time-like curve.

"We know time dilation is working in the forward direction. Perhaps we're seeing some Bohmian mechanics at work here," she suggested.

She remembered some of the work she'd read about in her recent studies.

"There's some very interesting work being done of the grounds that black holes are a misinterpretation of an exact special relativity solution," she said.

"Perhaps the equation describing inertial frame-dragging in the Kerr Metric is a time-space wave state equal and opposite to our precise degree of time dilation in an accelerated frame" she speculated.

"Yes, that's an interesting idea," Karl said.

"Remember when Susan Everett first came up with her temporal equation and she was using six dimensions, which we ended up compactifying into five? What if all six really are required? Perhaps there's something like two enantiomorphic universes with opposite arrows of time," she mused. "What appears to be a hole between these universes is more correctly described as an axial toroidal hypersurface (almost like a spool shape) that, at first glance, looks like a 'black hole.' At second glance, it may look like two 'universes,' but this too would be a misinterpretation.

"In that course I took, there was a model that worked

that way, you know. Closer examination revealed it to be a single toroidal surface. Rather than the universe being a flat surface deformed by gravity, you would see a single multi-D hypersurface with a helix-like twist and complexity algorithms appearing on the radial axis."

"Very cool," he agreed.

"And that's like our accelerator," she said. "It's accelerating the 'throat' of that toroidal hypersurface. It's that event horizon that produces the effect that looks like a black hole—but doesn't require the insane power requirements an actual black hole would, according to the current, incorrect equation. That's the part Susan figured out."

"Counteracting the Cherenkov radiation was vital, too," Karl reminded her.

"For sure," she agreed. "I think that was George's routine."

"It's as if we're back at the resting state on the surface and we're starting at the pole.

"We were trying to solve the wrong problem. Our qubits couldn't do the temporal communication that was required, but the principle of quantum teleportation—with a zero distance—does work, as it turns out. Well played, ASTRA.

"So, theoretically, things should be different, otherwise we'd be stuck in a causality loop."

"I hope you don't say *that* again."

"Using fractals as a qubit error correction carrier, using self-similar redundancies for error correction. It's quite elegant. And absolutely full of spirals."

"'It's all math' as Susan would often say."

"Since energy and mass are equivalent, the Planck constant

relates mass to frequency. The researchers back in 1947 were taking two high-frequency waveforms and exclusive-or'ing them together to derive a differential wave and then isolating and amplifying harmonic overtones in that phase-shifted frequency series. That was how they were getting the high frequencies needed without emitting huge amounts of heat or radiation."

"And we successfully synced to it once, that time the lab accident happened."

"Yes, and I think the mirage effect that was reported over Mount Rainier at the time was also due to a partial success."

"I think the algorithm set up our 25th-century electrons to be entangled with the electrons produced by their 20th-century quantum radar experiment and this produced the Alcubierre effect during what is usually called a waveform collapse. Our resonant entanglement collapsed the field back at the point where those entangled qubits were first enabled using the army's experimental algorithm—hence, the effect appeared back in 1947, at the source."

"If only I could… hey, wait a tick. Maybe *that's* the reason this isn't working. What if I need to target that exact moment in time? It worked then because the value happened to match a time-vector that aligned with the Fibonacci sequence. But now, we've got that code that can add different values together to target any specific time. I've been wasting my time trying to replicate the original experiment. Perhaps I just need to calculate the exact value that reaches back exactly to that moment in time where the team was doing their experiment and broadcasting their signal in 1947."

"Do we even know that?"

"Yes! That data was published in the report by the Project Looking Glass workgroup in the 21st century. 2018, I think it was. Shouldn't be too hard to find."

"I'll get to work on it."

25

The Valley of Decision

His name is Timeless, In the Sun.
He made the paths connected.
Time was All but In the Sun
saw Truth in light projected.

By 2454, jump tech had become ubiquitous enough that it was being used in industrial processes. After the first rounds of hardware and process simulations had been analyzed, it was common for installations to go through accelerated testing and calibration routines. These procedures benefitted greatly both in efficiency and accuracy by jump tech.

In America, NASA spun off an industrial provider of the technology. Known as JTI Jump Tech Innovations, it operated primarily as a space-based contractor for any instances where time displacement was beneficial to the bottom line of space-based businesses.

Terraformers, space-based crystal, mineral and biotech grow ops, interplanetary shippers, distillers, and every other kind of business in which there was a 'do nothing' period between the signing of the contract and the delivery of the product or service were the primary customers. Space itself was the killer app for jump tech.

Marjorie was in high orbit around the moon, working on calibrating the Deepvue 2 space telescope in August of 2454, when the news of the coming war on earth broke out. Although the war hadn't actually begun yet, the news outlets focused on the emergence of backchannel tech as indisputable proof that the war was all but inescapable.

Reaction to the news was sudden and severe. Mass panic ensued in Europe and the Middle East, where the war was predicted to begin. Even in the Americas, where modern-day prophets like Ty Thom had been popular figures in the media just thirty years ago, the general populace now accepted that looking into the future was the stuff of science, not prophecy. They may not have understood how it worked, but they believed it. And if the tea leaves said a war was coming, they believed that, too.

The conflict, it was claimed, would start in "The Luminous City." This was widely taken to mean Medina, the second holy city of Islam.

The news outlets scrambled to identify the first time backchannel tech might have been used for this sort of prognostication. Some named Ty Thom, the Tangler. Others pointed to the writings of the prophetic Havenite leader known as Saros. But the oldest verifiable instances anyone could name came from the years 2038 through 2046, in the form of Pastebin archives published under the title "Tales from Tomorrow" and attributed to a mysterious figure known as "Won Yong Han." It was he (or she?) who first prophesied the Omega Event that occurred on January 18, 2038, exactly as predicted.

"Marjorie, we're thinking of ending your mission early. There's a bit of a political situation happening down here and, well, we think it might be quite serious."

"What's going on?"

The mission controller explained the situation. Part of the problem was that France was a partner in the project and the country's responses to the emerging threat in the Middle East had made that partnership suddenly look less desirable than the American government wanted.

"I'm almost done here," she protested. "Why don't I just finish the work and then check in? If it's going to be a shooting match down there, honestly, I think I'd rather be up here. Are they going to drop nukes, or what?"

"No word of nukes, specifically, but it has been characterized as a war that starts in the middle east—in Saudi Arabia, specifically. Could get messy."

"Look, tell them I want to stay, and I'll jump ahead if necessary to avoid any conflict that's going on down there. Wars don't last forever."

"This is the Middle East we're talking about, remember—where wars last *almost* forever."

"Well, good luck to y'all down there. Let me know how to proceed, okay?"

"Will do, Deepvue. Over and out."

Deepvue was a mission that Marjorie had championed as a peacetime hero project. There had been so many controversies and so much bad publicity over what NASA and ASTRA had been up to over the past thirty years, she wanted to set a good example and get behind something clearly designed for leading-edge scientific research.

Moral leadership, too, seemed more important than ever after information leaked out about ASTRA's role in the secret deployment of American space-based weapons. Suddenly, ASTRA's name seemed to come up every time the media was looking for an example of the space program's damaged reputation.

* * *

Did You Know?

The Deepvue telescope—or more correctly, telescopic array—is unique in that it is made up of two or more separate but complementary Beryllium mirror modules designed to work together to create a longer effective focal length than would be practical to create with a single reflector or lens array alone. Containing 36 mirrors in all, the Deepvue array is the largest and most sophisticated telescopic array ever launched into space.

* * *

Marjorie flew out to meet the Deepvue following its initial insertion into lunar orbit. Orbiting the moon as opposed to the earth offered several advantages, including a solution for the so-called 'shuttle glow' and the foreground ultraviolet light of the geocorona. Other key advantages were the greater sky coverage afforded by high lunar orbit and the lower orbital velocity. The greatest benefit of lunar orbit was the ability to observe close to the sun for much longer periods of time than those of an earth-orbiting space telescope. And monitoring the sun had become a key priority for NASA.

The calibration of the telescopic array was an ideal application for the Starjumper tech. Once the lunar orbit insertion sequence was completed, Marjorie got the commissioning phase underway. This phase, which usually takes about 60 days, and the subsequent polar mapping phase, which can take at least a year, were able to be completed in a fraction of the usual time thanks to the elimination of the "do nothing" periods following each calibration step. Instead of taking at least 14 months, Marjorie was able to do 16 months' worth of calibration work in 16 days.

* * *

Within hours of the August 3 release of the report of the coming war, the news was being hotly debated in the executive office of the White House. The president's advisors said they considered it a credible threat and urged him to call a meeting with the joint chiefs of staff.

"This thing is supposed to happen in 21 days? That doesn't give us a lot of wiggle room, now, does it?"

"No sir. However, it is a well-known military tactic to drive a poor decision and thus weaken a defensive position by setting an arbitrarily short deadline. That may be what we are seeing play out here."

"What evidence do we have that this source is credible, general?" asked the president.

"This came through an NSA[4]-certified secure backchannel from the NASA jumpstation facility in Houston, sir. It is, however, not the only source of this report. An earlier account of a similar nature was attributed to Russian sources ahead of our initial receipt of the information."

"So, the Russians supplied this information?"

"No sir. A CIA field agent by the name of Surya Byrne was the corroborating source. She has restricted access to the Houston jumpstation facility and is believed to have independently confirmed the time, location, and other details of the earlier report."

"But we're not sure if this information is accurate?"

"She's an experienced jumper who has worked closely with several of the original developers of the technology we're using to get this information, so she's a credible source."

"Do we have any tangible proof?"

"No sir. We're working on that."

"We can't act on rumors like that."

"Of course, sir. We'll do everything we can to firm up our intelligence on this matter, *asap*."

[4] National Security Agency

Immediately upon hearing this statement from the president, the joint chiefs took an extremely skeptical view of any other suggestions.

The director of national security took a different tack. "As you may know, sir, a moratorium on altering the flow of events in the natural timeline based on information from the future was declared by president Harry Truman back in 1947, based on credible scientific evidence that any and all such action constituted a significant risk to the American way of life. I believe the time has come to reexamine that moratorium, as it now appears that there is a credible risk that exactly the opposite situation may occur if we do *not* take decisive actions at this time.

"In short, sir, I recommend that we do everything we can to put a cap on this war before it begins. I recommend that you use those existing jumpstation facilities to send intelligence agents, SWAT teams, Navy SEALs or, hell, anyone else who might stand half a chance at avoiding another world war."

"What makes you think things are so different now that it's safe to try altering the future?"

"Back in 1947, one of the leading theoretical quantum physicists of the day, a man by the name of Dr. Hans Bethe, was asked about the risks. His logic was: 'if we do nothing, we know what will happen. If we try to change that, we lose that certainty and risk something much worse.' That situation is reversed today, and the risk of dire consequences is far more acute if we elect to do nothing. We have a report that a war—maybe a big one—is about to start in the Middle East. We do know that, if we do nothing, a report of this event will be sent to us. If things were due to get a lot worse than that, I believe we would have been advised of those subsequent events. I believe this situation demands that we *do* act to preserve the peace, as is the American way. The benefits attempting to ensure a peaceful outcome clearly outweigh the risks. We must be brave to reap the harvest in this valley of decision."

"Seems to make sense to me, Mr. President, that we gather some more intelligence from the field. We know where the conflict starts and when. We should have as many eyes on the ground on the Saudi situation as possible."

The president thought for a moment. "Let's find a few subject matter experts in to weigh in on this situation. Get me a few of the people who've actually done this sort of reporting from the future, and a few who would be willing to jump forward a couple of weeks to help us keep the peace over there. I want people with experience in war reporting and strategic analysis to get in there and tell us why this, uh, *storm* is brewing. And if you can track down the people who actually invent stuff like this, all the better."

"We'll get right on it, sir."

* * *

The phone rang in the intelligence office. The executive assistant answered, then put the call on hold and messaged her boss. "It's the director of national security, sir."

"Jamison here. Hello, sir. Yes, I've got a list of candidates right here in front of me. We've broken them into two groups: one for the reporting work the president requested, and another with specific expertise in time-jumping technologies.

No sir, we haven't reached out to all of them yet. Thought you might like to have some input on that. I certainly will, sir. Thank you."

On Jamison's screen was the list of candidates and their roles.

Reporting

Surya Byrne – CIA agent, surveillance specialist

Chaissie Morrow – News reporter, jump specialist

Andrew Stern – Astronaut, Qm reporter

Marjorie Blint – Astronaut, astrophysicist

Technical

George Gunderson – Qm programmer, developer

Karl Schraeder – Engineer, ASTRA tech expert

Li Yan Zhang – Engineer, temporal tech expert

Emil Fidor – Quantum physicist, temporal tech

Moments after he sent the list to the director of national security, a reply appeared, with the name Surya Byrne circled. *I definitely want her in the mix*, said the attached note. *She can keep an eye on the others, maybe even lead the team.*

* * *

26

The Secret Mission

The quadcopter landed on the driveway in front of Surya's house. A man in uniform jumped out and approached the house. The front door opened and Surya stepped out onto the front porch, shielding her eyes from the wind.

"Surya?" he said.

"Yes." she said, holding on to her windblown hair with one hand as she pulled the door closed with the other.

"I'm General Jamison. We spoke earlier."

"Ready to go?" he shouted over the whine of the blades. She nodded and hoisted the blue sport bag she carried. "Is this okay to bring?" she asked.

"Just stash it under your seat while we're in flight; it should be fine," he said. The automatic door swung open and he helped her into her seat in the passenger area before climbing into the front seat. "Put one of these on," he said, gesturing to his headset. "And fasten your seatbelt!"

The first thing she heard when she put on her headset was

a familiar voice. She felt a hand on her shoulder. "Hello Surya, long time no see." She turned and there was Chaissie in the seat directly behind her. Beside Chaissie sat Dr. Emil Fidor.

"Sorry about that situation in Beijing," Chaissie said. "We tried to take good care of you. But..."

"Hey, no worries," said Surya. "I never got a chance to thank you or Mister Thom for the hospitality. Hello Dr. Fidor. Nice to see you again."

Chaissie leaned forward and spoke quietly. "For the record, I resigned over the inappropriate way you were treated."

"At least we got to see Beijing, huh?"

Whether or not Chaissie and Nolan had known more about her than they let on at the time didn't matter much now. She wasn't going to let on that she knew Mister Thom's true identity unless Chaissie or Emil brought it up. And if they knew the real reason she was on the team today, they weren't letting on either.

* * *

The quadcopter descended from the haze hanging over Novelty Hill and set down at the Redmond Ridge helipad.

The uniformed man led Surya, Chaissie and Emil to a nearby building and unlocked the door with a passkey.

He led them to a conference room inside. There, behind the gleaming glass walls, sat Karl and Li Yan.

"They haven't been able to talk to George yet, but he's got all those agents handling his communications, so he's probably aware that he's.... Wait. He says he's online now."

"Well, he's right on time then," said Li Yan, looking at the clock. "How unusual."

As George's video stream initialized, a pair of audio-only feeds named Andrew and Marjorie appeared below it.

"Can you hear us okay?" said Marjorie.

"Loud and clear," said Li Yan. "Where are you?"

"Heh, Andrew and I are about 700 kilometers above the Schrödinger crater on the far side of the moon, down by the South Pole."

Li Yan put up her hand when three men in military fatigues entered the room and sat down at the table. "Sorry, who are these people?"

"These are your military support personnel. If anything goes wrong, their job is to take care of you and steer you clear of any danger. They are also well-versed in weapons handling, as we do not have time to teach you all those skills in the deadly arts of hand-to-hand combat in the limited time we have available."

"We've got a lot to cover today, so I'll get right to it. We are operating at the direct order of the Commander In Chief on a mission that will be classified as top secret. As such you will all be required to commit to absolute secrecy, should you decide to participate in this service to your country. Although I cannot disclose the details of this mission to you until that commitment has been confirmed, I can tell you that you have been selected because we believe you all are the right people for this mission. In short, we need you. Is there anyone here who does not wish to sign a strict non-disclosure agreement, which is required of you before any further disclosures are made?"

Dr. Fidor raised his hand. "I'm not an American citizen," he said.

"We know that sir, and we welcome your participation due to your expertise in, well, let's just leave it at that for now."

"I can promise you we'll do our very best to keep you safe and help you succeed."

"All right. Here is the form we need you to sign. To be perfectly clear, you are agreeing that you will deny any and all government involvement in any actions you will undertake during this mission. You hereby agree that any and all risks you may take and the consequences thereof, if any, are your sole responsibility. Sign here and here. And here. Thank you. Commander Sand?"

One of the SEALs stood up and walked to the podium. Good afternoon, my name is Sand. I'm the tactical planner for this mission. It's my job to get you in and out of the city of Medina as safely as possible.

"You'll notice that I did *not* say 'without incident.' In fact, I fully expect there to be some complications, so we've made sure to have backups of all critical components, including the configuration of your teams. We're organizing this effort as two groups, each of which has two roles.

So, we've got two people assigned a role, allowing you some flexibility in how the teams operate, in case some members are separated from the others or otherwise indisposed."

The screen showed the Reporting and Technical group members. "Here they are," he said.

Reporting

Surya Byrne – CIA agent, surveillance specialist

Chaissie Morrow – News reporter, jump specialist

Andrew Stern – Astronaut, Qm reporter

Marjorie Blint – Astronaut, astrophysicist

Technical

George Gunderson – Qm programmer, developer

Karl Schraeder – Engineer, ASTRA tech expert

Li Yan Zhang – Engineer, temporal tech expert

Emil Fidor – Quantum physicist, temporal tech

"Now, you folks know each other's personalities better than we do, so here's how we're going to do it: we want two teams, each with two from the 'reporter' group and two from the 'technical' group. And this is just an example, but let's say that Andrew and Marjorie decide they want to work together. They will pair up with two people from the technical side. I'm going to give you guys five minutes to decide. Any questions?"

Five minutes later, Surya held up her hand. "We're done," she said. "This is what we came up with."

On the table in front of her were two groups of name cards.

"These are our picks for 'A' team, and this is 'B' team."

On 'A' team, Surya was paired with George and Chaissie with Emil. The 'B' team paired Andrew with Marjorie and Karl with Li Yan.

"All right, good work," said Sand. "Here's the plan. The

'A' group will jump forward thirteen-point-five days and will arrive in Medina first, acting as primary mission operatives under my command. The 'B' group will follow when Stern and Blint have returned from orbit, on or around day six. In my absence, Surya is designated as your overall mission leader, as I believe she is the only one who has been in the Medina area of Saudi Arabia before. Please correct me if I'm wrong about that."

The others were silent.

"All right. Now, I want you folks on B team to decide which one of you is going to be the leader for your team. This is the person from whom you will obey orders—and that person will report to me. You've got two minutes to decide." He stood like a statue with his hands clasped behind his back for two minutes straight.

"Time's up. What have we got?"

"We choose Li Yan Zhang."

Li Yan smiled ruefully and said, "Apparently, I'm the only one on the team who has read *The Art of War*."

Karl didn't say anything else once the decision was made, but he knew, perhaps better than any of them, that she was a great choice when the job demanded ruthless decision making.

"All right. Surya and Li Yan will both report to me. Li Yan, you will obey orders and take direction from Surya, and you all will obey the orders they give you. Anyone have a problem with that?"

Everyone sat silently.

"Great. Schraeder and Zhang: The plan is for 'B' team

is to set up camp at Victory Base and continue to gather intel on any and all situations that may emerge during that thirteen-day period following the 'A' team's initial jump from the Russian station at Volgograd. Following their jump to day thirteen at Volgograd, the 'A' team will be delivered to the Medina area, where they will act as our primary operatives in this mission. Stern and Blint are expected to arrive back from lunar orbit and will rendezvous with you on or around day six at Victory Base. The assembled 'B' team will then be moved to the Medina area or the Volgograd jumpstation should time-line advancement or personnel changes be required."

"Why Volgograd?"

"Most importantly, it's the closest one to our target destination, and it's the only jumpstation we've been authorized to use. We think there's one in Moscow, too, but they said *nyet* to that one. Volgograd is about seventeen hundred clicks due north of our base in Baghdad.

"We'll be flying you in and out of the area via our joint operations base at the Victory Base Complex near the Baghdad international airport. This location will allow us to get support to you as needed, and to expedite your departure at the conclusion of the mission.

"We have transports stationed there available for our use around the clock there, and of course Iraq is right on the border of Saudi Arabia, so that is a priority as well.

"Morrow and Stern: you will each carry a Qm transponder with you at all times and Morrow will communicate status every four hours and before taking any action. We will relocate the backchannel transponder to Victory Base to facilitate communications with 'A' team during the period prior to Stern's arrival.

"A team: you will have no more than 68 hours after your arrival to complete your mission. We will supply your team leaders with intel from our agents in the field now and we also have a team at Brookhaven working on getting you as much information as possible about all aspects of the threat scenario and the actors involved. We will pull you out of there four hours before the war is slated to begin, at the very latest."

"Forgive me for asking," said Fidor, "but if time is of the essence to this mission, why not utilize the full time we have available and send both teams into Medina at the same time, rather than skip fourteen days of potentially valuable reconnaissance time for half of the team?"

"Great question, and to be honest with you, we did a lot of thinking about the situation and seriously considered doing just that. However, we already have people working that way and, frankly, they're not seeing a lot of success yet. We feel that having two teams working together in two separate time periods and communicating future events via the Qm backchannel we think gives us a better chance at beating the odds. The more the 'A' team can tell us about the hours leading up to the initiation of hostilities, the better we can prepare the 'B' team for those eventualities. Being able to act with reliable intel about future events gives us a strategic advantage that has never been part of the playbook before."

That's not entirely true, thought Surya, but she kept her mouth shut.

"I see. Thank you," said Fidor.

Sand put down the pointer and gripped the edges of the podium.

"I assume it goes without saying that it is very important that you keep your team leaders informed of any and all actions you intend to take. And it is *critical* that you team leaders keep us informed. We will supply you with all the identification, clothing and equipment you will need. Any questions?"

"Please be ready for travel to Volgograd from this location at 0800 hours Pacific time on August 7th. If you cannot be here at the Novelty Hill pick-up point at that time, you will not be able to participate and your absence may jeopardize the mission. Is that understood?"

No one in the room said anything, but they all nodded and George sent a thumbs up emoji. Finally, to break the uncomfortable silence, Marjorie said "Roger that."

"All right. Thank you all and good luck. We will be in touch."

* * *

One day earlier...
Karl and Li Yan were awakened by the sound of knocking on their hotel room door.

"Just a minute," yelled Li Yan, slipping into a hotel robe. She straightened her hair and looked through the peep-hole. It was Commander Sand. She opened the door. "Good morning."

"Sorry to bother you before breakfast, but I wanted to get

this to you *asap.*" He held up a rectangular metal flight case by its handle. "May I come in?"

"We're not really, uh...."

"It's fine," said Karl, now in his shirt and pants. Sand entered the room and set the flight case on the chair. He unbuckled the latches and pulled out a Qmunications transceiver.

"Thank you again for agreeing to help us out. I wonder if I could ask a little favor of you. You are familiar with these Qmunicator modules, I assume?"

Li Yan nodded; Karl said, "Ya, very familiar. What do you need?"

"Well," said Sand. "This module is linked to the one that we will be sending forward with the other team, as I mentioned in our briefing yesterday afternoon. Could you help us run a few tests before we get started, to make sure that the modules are working correctly?"

"Sure, what kind of testing do you want to do?"

"Nothing too complicated. We just want to be sure your teammates will be able to reliably transmit reports every four hours or when there's breaking news. And maybe you can help us set up some basic notifications to alert a user when a message arrives, or something like that. That's doable, right?"

"No problem," Karl assured him. "Everybody on the team is pretty familiar with how these things work. I can help you with all of that. I'll set it up and run the diagnostic to make sure the automatic notifications are working properly. If you want, I can set it to send brief messages acknowledging receipt after each one comes in—or whatever else you might need."

"That sounds perfect, thanks. I'll see you at breakfast, yeah?"

"Ya," said Karl. "We'll be there at 8 o'clock sharp."

* * *

27

Hero City

At 0800 on August 7th, everyone on the 'A' and 'B' teams except Marjorie and Andrew had convened in the smart-windowed entranceway to the Novelty Hill conference center with their duffel bags, packsacks, coffee cups and water bottles. There they waited until at last they heard the crescendoing roar of the quadcopter landing on the helipad outside. Commander Sand appeared at the conference room door and waved them outside and onto the 'copter.

After the takeoff whine of the engines diminished, Sand detailed the next steps. "We'll be transferring to a transport plane at the SeaTac airport for the sixteen-hour flight to Volgograd. You may wish to get some sleep during that time, as it will be 10 a.m. local time tomorrow when we arrive in Volgograd, at which time I will escort Team Alpha to the Volga jumpstation, where they will jump ahead thirteen days.

"Following our jump, Team Alpha will be put onto a plane and taken to the Madinah airport, where an agent will accompany you to your hotel room and ensure that the Qm devices are operating as designed and that there are no other unforeseen difficulties. In short, we'll make sure you're all set up and comfortable there in Medina.

"Team Beta will, meanwhile, be camped at our base just north of the city. They will avail themselves of our support and intel services at Victory Base until day thirteen, when they will join the other team in Medina. In both cases, everything you will need, including appropriate clothing, identification, local currency and transportation to take you from there to the Al Madinah Hotel, will be provided. For security reasons, a written itinerary will *not* be provided. However, your clothing has labels which contain a very simple sequence of numbers indicating which pieces are designed to go together —everything that starts with a 'three', for example, is part of an ensemble that should be worn together. The second number indicates how many pieces are part of that ensemble. Hopefully, that will be enough to get you started, as this is not my particular area of expertise. If you *do* have a fashion emergency, let your team leader know, and we will attempt to reduce your potential for embarrassment.

"On a related topic, it's very important that you are respectful of the Muslim culture. Islamic people are very sensitive to this and, in fact, non-Muslims are not even supposed to set foot inside the mosque. Please do your best to be reverent, watch carefully, and do as those around you do. This is their holy place, the tomb of their prophet, and we are trying to preserve it for them. We want to stop the bad guys from blowing it up. We most certainly do not want to *be* the bad guys."

He handed out a one-page list of clothing and local customs guidelines. "They are pretty strict about their traditions," noted Sand. "For example, the local custom is shoes off before entering religious institutions. No short pants, no gold bracelets or necklaces, et cetera. I want you to adhere to these guidelines without exception. Ladies, please pay particular attention to the rather long list of restrictions that apply to you.

"Your hotel in Medina is about a five-minute walk from the reported site of the terrorist attack. It's an area of the mosque known as the Green Dome, said to be the final resting place of the prophet Muhammed. That's the target of the bomber that sets off the chain of events that leads to war.

"So, it's pretty clearly a radical anti-Islamic individual or group we're looking for. But first things first."

He looked at his watch. "We should be at the Seattle Tacoma airport in roughly eight minutes. When we get into that transport plane, I want y'all to get some sleep. It's a long flight."

* * *

Unlike the quadcopter, there were no noise-canceling headsets provided on the transport. Still, the familiar jet engine noise was unobtrusive enough to be tolerable. No one was sleepy for the first half of the trip, but by the time they were in the middle of the Atlantic, it was dark outside and everyone was doing their best to at least look like they were sleeping.

George was busy organizing his agents to search for flights into Medina that correlated with van or truck rentals, weapons or ammunition purchases, hotel room rentals, anti-Muslim posts or videos, currency transfers, searches for the phrase "green dome," and dozens of other fuzzy search key phrases.

As the plane neared its sixteenth hour in the air, Sand checked the time. "All right," he said. "We should be landing in a few minutes. It is 10:00 a.m. local time. There will be ten minutes for bathroom breaks and quick snacks after we disembark. Alpha team, you're with me. Good luck, Beta team. We'll see you in Medina in a couple of weeks.

* * *

When they cleared customs, Sand and the Alpha team were met in the Arrivals area by a man holding a sign with a large 'S' on it. He introduced himself as Alexi and led them outside to a white van.

After a 30-minute ride in the van from the airport to Volgograd State University, the van pulled into the parking lot of a rather nondescript gray concrete building remarkable only for the pair of very large doors at the front of the building. It looked like it might be a Brutalist architecture-style firehall. "This is it," said Alexi.

"Thanks," said Sand. "See you later."

Inside the building, Sand and the Alpha team members had to show their ID to a guard at the front desk. He picked up the phone. A moment later, a middle-aged man in a white labcoat arrived at the desk and led them down a flight of stairs to the Volga accelerator research project.

He looked at the old doctor and smiled. "Ah, you must be Dr. Fidor. Welcome. It is a great honor to meet you. My name is Dr. Maksim Popov. Don't worry. I know you have a different name on your ID. We are happy to help you. Your team has a good chance, I hope, of averting something big, and we want to support you in this noble effort. So, we're going to be good friends for a few minutes and then we will send you off. How does that sound, Commander?"

Sand glanced at his watch and gave them a thumbs up.

Dr. Popov sat next to Emil. "It's wonderful that you can be here. We read about you in school. You can understand me, with my accent, I hope?"

"Very well," said Fidor graciously. "Thank you for asking. I wish the circumstances weren't so urgent. I should very much like to learn more about what you are doing here."

"Of course. Let me give you the two-minute tour, right this way," said Dr. Popov. He led Emil to a set of control desks next to a circular platform. Above it, surrounded by cables and conduits, was an imposingly large white structure that looked like a lenticular cloud or, more fancifully, like a flying saucer. It was far more dramatic looking than anything he'd seen in China or America. "This is VARP, he said. I hope it doesn't look too familiar to you."

"Not at all. It's wonderful," Emil said, genuinely awed.

"Dr. Popov lowered his voice. "I wonder if you might invite me to your lab in America sometime? I should very much like to see that."

"I will see what I can do. I would like that, too."

They heard Sand calling from the next room.

"Ah, I think that means our time is up. Well, best of luck to you all."

* * *

For security reasons, the American tactical planners insisted that the teams bring their own Qmunications transponders, so the first thing they did was to run a quick one-minute test to make sure that the American Qm modules were compatible with the Russian jump gate.

When the module reappeared after sixty seconds, George selected the ROM-based test sequence and hit send. Sand studied the output on the receiving module. So far so good. He sent the test response and was relieved to see that two-way communications were working exactly as they should.

"Good news, team," he announced. "You are cleared to go." They reset the modules and shuffled everyone on the A team into the Russian transit pod, with their suitcases of clothing, weapons, and supplies. It wasn't clear to anyone why Sand was bringing the weapons through the gate as well, but he did.

"Is everyone ready?" asked Dr. Popov's voice over the radio. Surya looked at Emil, George and Chaissie, all buckled into the semi-circular stand-up module.

"Ready," confirmed Surya and the initialization phase sequence began.

It was an interesting design, thought Fidor. One could configure one, two, or three of the 120-degree angled segments, each of which could accommodate up to four people. The modules swiveled to provide easy access to a central pylon, where the supplies were placed on upper and lower sets of meter-high racks per module. Really efficient, he thought.

Blink.

The time display jumped forward and the status indicators on the frame turned green. The technicians instantly changed places at their control desks.

"Everything functioned properly," said Popov proudly. "Let me help you unlock these frames." He lifted the armrest and the whole frame opened up like a curved refrigerator door, revealing the storage racks behind it.

"Grab your gear," barked Sand. "We've got a plane to catch."

* * *

The Green Dome

The transport plane carrying Alpha team lifted off from Volgograd airport and headed due south toward Baghdad, with an estimated flight time, the captain said, of two hours and thirty-eight minutes. Chaissie and Emil sat together and beside them sat Surya and George.

Emil was very talkative and spent much of the flight chatting with Chaissie on a wide variety of topics, ranging from favorite pets to best places to eat. When he found out that she had visited Switzerland there was no stopping him.

George was very interested in his work at CERN on projects such as the High Luminosity Large Hadron Collider, which had laid the groundwork for some of his own development efforts.

Emil, too, was interested in learning more about George's breakthrough work that allowed the HELX accelerator to outperform much larger circular accelerators. Compensating for the effects of Cherenkov radiation had been a problem that he had also struggled with.

Every time a network signal became available, George apologized for the interruption and checked his agents' status. But the 'signal available' notifications grew increasingly infrequent as they traveled south over Georgia and Armenia.

"That's the Turkish border down there," noted the pilot, "and, to your right, you'll see the snowy peaks of Mount Samdi, or Samdi Dağ as it's known to the locals. And just beyond that is the Iraqi border. We will be landing in Baghdad in approximately thirty-five minutes."

When the plane landed, George lagged behind the others in disembarking, so pleased he was to have connectivity again.

"You've got a connecting flight to catch," Sand reminded him. George sifted through his agents' findings.

They crossed the apron and boarded the small electric plane that would take them from Baghdad to Medina. It was an older model, with civil registration markings. Thankfully, models like these were much quieter than the big turbofan engines used on high-altitude long-distance flights.

"We will be landing in Medina in a little less than five hours," Sand announced. "Get some rest."

* * *

It was 6 p.m. by the time the plane had landed at the Madinah airport. "Well," said Emil as he stepped into the sweltering heat and glare of the late afternoon sun, "That is certainly enough air travel for one day. It's good to be back on the ground." He loosened his tie. "Whew. Warm, though."

Chaissie and the others followed him down the steps from the plane and they stood on the hot apron waiting for Sand to disembark. He was visible through the cockpit window, talking with the pilot. A moment later, he bounded down the steps and pointed to a white van parked nearby. "Put your stuff in the van and get in. I'll be with y'all in a minute."

The pilot emerged from the plane and opened the cargo bay door on the fuselage. Sand helped him unload a large and heavy-looking case from the cargo bay and they carried it over to the rear of the van, where the driver stood near the open rear doors. They slid the case into the vehicle and slammed the door. Sand shook the pilot's hand, then opened the passenger-side door and slid into the passenger seat next to the driver. "Okay," Sand said to the driver. "We're ready to go now."

It took another fifteen minutes to travel from the Medina airport to the hotel.

"Oh, I hope there's a restaurant near the hotel," said Surya who, like Chaissie, was clad in a modest gown covering her knees and shoulders. "I'm starving."

"They do," said George. "Apparently it's 'healthy' food."

"I'll settle for anything that doesn't kill me right now," she said.

The van pulled off the expressway onto a wide road lined with upscale hotels. "This is your hotel here," said the driver. The van pulled into the portico area of the Al Madinah and stopped.

Sand jumped out and slid open the side door. "Please bring your own bag with you and follow me." The driver stood behind the van watching as they followed Sand into the hotel lobby. He then climbed back into the van and drove away.

The air-conditioned lobby was a welcome change from the sweltering heat outside, and the reception desk provided both human- and machine-translation options. They were able to check in without incident. Sand arranged to pay for five separate rooms. "Let me know if any of these rooms aren't being occupied and we'll put them to good use," he said.

They carried their own bags up to their rooms and agreed to meet in forty-five minutes in the restaurant on the premises.

Sand picked up the house phone. "I'd like to make a reservation for five...."

* * *

Forty-five minutes later, the five of them were all dressed in traditional Saudi eveningwear and looking as though they had just stepped out of a shower. "No work discussions at the table," Sand quietly reminded them.

After a tasty meal of kabsa, mutabbaq, and shawarma, the waiters brought them a plate of complimentary *maamul* short breads. "These are excellent with coffee or tea," noted Sand. After they were finished, Sand invited them to his room for a brief meeting.

"As I won't be able to keep constant tabs on all of you, I'm going to spend some time with each of you, working toward specific objectives. Let's meet here every morning to discuss those at 8:00 a.m. and every evening at 8:00 p.m. As I'm sure you can probably imagine, it is critically important that, under no circumstances, should you discuss or disclose any part of the mission, or your real names to anyone outside our team. From now on, you must use your alias identity names only. I recommend you do this in public and in private for security purposes.

"So, figure out the clothing you'll be wearing tomorrow and have a good rest. I'll see you here at 8:00 a.m. sharp. We'll have breakfast right after that."

George checked the agents' status. Mosque attendance was estimated as 82% below normal, due to elevated risk factors, with a 394% greater risk of detection of any unusual on-site activity. Indeed, one needed only to look out the hotel window to see the greatly increased presence of police and military vehicles in the area.

Chaissie knocked on Emil's door. "I don't feel too good about going into the mosque if we're not supposed to go in there, you know? I probably shouldn't have agreed to do that."

"Come in and close the door," said Emil. "Please, sit down."

* * *

Surya knocked on George's door. "Can I come in?"

"I never really got a chance to apologize for disappearing when we were in Beijing."

"Yeah, that really was kind of upsetting. I didn't know if you were alive or dead."

"I'm sorry. I got so intimidated by them. They were asking all these personal questions. I told them I had to leave.

I should have let you know right away what was going on, I'm sorry."

"Hey, stuff happens. I was relieved to learn that you were okay, we both got to see Beijing, and I made some money. I hope you had a nice time while you were there. I never did get to meet Mister Thom after all those promises, by the way, so I think that whole angle might have been a sham, anyway."

"Do you know why he never showed his face?" Surya asked. "Perhaps I should rephrase that. Do you *want* to know why he never showed his face?"

"Oh, you are wondering whether I knew that the mysterious Mister Thom was really our old acquaintance Nolan Stern? And how Nolan's two assistants both ended up working for Thom? Or how Fidor came into possession of the accelerator design licensed to Nolan Stern? Yeah, I put two and two together. Fairly obvious, really. And then some investigative news report confirmed it."

"Yeah. Chaissie told me about it, too."

"He sounds like a real rat."

* * *

Chaissie and Emil, dressed in cool Egyptian cotton, were already at the table in the restaurant when the others arrived. Like the rest of the team, they'd already been given multiple reminders about not talking about locations or other plans in public. And, like the others on the team, they had been instructed to use only their assigned identities when conversing in public.

Surya was Sonya, George was Joel, Chaissie was Cheri

and Emil was Eli. Commander Sand was Sam. And, when the other team showed up in 12 days, they'd be referring to Andrew as Anton, Marjorie as Marnie, Karl as Karim and Li Yan as Lily.

The others were making small talk around the table when Chaissie veered right into forbidden topic territory. "I've been using the AI to study scenarios and participants ranked most likely to be willing to take radical action of the nature reported in that Qmunication about the coming war," she whispered.

Surya glared at her and put a finger to her lips. Chaissie continued, and even got a bit louder as she went along. "The AI started by establishing motives for various players and groups. One that came up, for example, was a group known as the Meccans—a mercantile Arab tribe known as the Quraysh. These people were in skirmishes and, later, at war with the Muslims for years, until they converted *en masse* to Islam around 630 CE. However, there have long been reports of secretive factions of dissenters appealing to the Quraishi's sense of honor and demanding that they fulfill their blood vengeance. There was," she said in a hushed voice, "a decisive battle between Muslims and Meccans known as The Day of the Criterion that, had things played out differently, might have greatly altered world history."

"The same can be said for many of history's quarrels," noted Emil.

"Yes," agreed Chaissie, "but this one, in particular, has been passed down in Islamic history as a decisive victory attributable to divine intervention." In a voice scarcely louder than a whisper, she added, "I am worried that what we are doing now, by potentially meddling with the timeline, might well be the same."

"I think we all share your concerns," said Emil, "but with millions of lives at stake, how can we not, in good conscience, take action?"

"I know we think we understand what's going on here," said George, "but there might be a simpler explanation. I've been studying the exact times and locations where the Qmunications reports came in and there appears to be a pattern. Look at this."

Surya interrupted. "Let's...discuss this on our way to the plaza, shall we?"

* * *

Emil couldn't understand why Chaissie had raised these issues in a public place, when they had specifically been told not to. "You were uncomfortable discussing this at the hotel?"

"I worry that the room might have been bugged. We really can't afford to take any chances."

She opened up the list George had forwarded to her, showing the messages received and the exact dates and times when they had been received.

"Location one: undisclosed location in Russia. All right, we know there is a jumpstation in Volgograd, so that's a possible source. Now look at the date: Aug 8. That's when we were there.

"Okay, next report: thirteen days, two hours and forty-five

minutes later. We were on the ground at Baghdad at that time.”

“Oh my,” said Emil. “I think I see where you’re going with this.”

“But we have the Qm modules. They are in our control. We’ve verified that what Alpha team sends, we receive, and vice versa.”

“Yes, but what if they are not the matched set we think they are? What if the receiving module for our Qm transponder is *not* in B team’s control, but in someone else’s—”

“Someone else’s?! Who are you thinking of?”

“I think it might be Sand,” said Emil quietly. “I’m not sure I trust that man.”

“Wait, wait. I’m confused. Why would Sand invite us along on a mission aimed at thwarting his own plan?”

“The only reason I can think of is that he might be using us as the patsies. Make it look like we—the time-traveling bad guys—are out to declare war on Islam. Rather convenient that all of the bad guys came into the country using false identities.”

Chaissie put a hand on her head as if to keep her jaw from dropping. “Maybe the idea is to make it look like *we* were trying to start the war and they will then ‘catch us in the act’ and come across looking like the good guys for, you know, reasons.”

“Maybe to avoid a real war between Saudi Arabia and whichever political entity is really behind this.”

“I don’t think it’s a war between Saudi Arabia and anyone. This is Al Madinah, the second holy city of Islam we are talking about. This is a religious war. Some kind of effort to disrupt Islamic dominance in the Middle East, perhaps? A Christian holy war?"

Emil sighed. "If you're on the right track," he said, "we might be at real risk here. They kill us, plant weapons on us, and boom, we go down in history as the ones who started the war."

"Ugh," moaned Chaissie. "I *knew* this was a bad idea."

"So, let me get this straight. You think someone on Sand's command team—or maybe even Sand himself—is replicating the message on their end to a second transponder and sending a *copy* to the B team module? And vice versa—when we send a reply to them, it's actually going somewhere else, and they can thus control exactly what is said, and what is seen and what isn't? Huh."

When Chaissie shared her concerns with George, he was quick to respond.

"I might be able to encode a message using a cryptographic method that Andrew came up with while we were inventing the Qmunications protocol. He'd probably recognize it—and it's doubtful anyone else would, at least right off the bat. That way, we can at least let the B team know what's going on."

"It's worth a try."

* * *

Karl stood on the balcony overlooking the green dome and mopped his blue forehead. "God, I don't know what I was thinking to agree to come here at the height of summer. It's positively sweltering."

Marjorie handed Andrew a printout of the encoded message. "*Pour vous*, Anton."

"*Merci.*" Marjorie put a finger to her lips and silently signaled to him to not say anything about the content of the message, in case the room was bugged.

Andrew gave her the thumbs-up sign and studied the page for a moment before a smile came to his face. It was easy to see that he recognized the code. He grabbed a pencil and began writing out the decoded characters.

A moment later, he held up the result for Marjorie and the others to see.

We think Sand is up to something, it read. *We are not going ahead with the plan.*

"Bah, I can't make any sense of that gibberish," he fibbed. "Must have been scrambled by that bug in the decoder. We'd better ask them to send it again."

Emil held up a hastily scribbled note. It said "I'm not comfortable about changing plans without discussing it with the others."

The others looked at each other nervously. "Come on, let's go for a walk," said Li Yan. They would be able to talk about this outside.

The Thirteenth Day

"What!?" barked Commander Sand when Surya told him the others had decided to back out of the plan.

"Where are they now?" he demanded to know.

"They're back in their rooms, packing," she said.

He opened the side table drawer and pulled out a gun, then stormed out of the room.

There was a knock on the door of Li Yan and Karl's room. Karl looked though the peephole. "It's Sand," he whispered. "He looks pissed."

"Better open it," said Li Yan.

Sand stormed into the room. "What the hell's going on, Zhang?" he said, looking at her accusingly.

"The name is *Lily*..." she said slowly, her eyes narrowing, "... and we just don't feel comfortable with the... plan."

"I don't give a shit whether you're comfortable or not," he said threateningly. "The time for backing out has long passed —we are one hundred per cent committed to this now."

"No, we're not," she replied defiantly.

He pulled the gun out from behind his back. "Yes you *are*."

Karl stepped in front of Li Yan and glared at Sand. "Fuck you. Go ahead and kill us. We'd rather see eight people die than a half a billion.

Sand sneered and waved the pistol dismissively. "Out of the way, you blue freak."

Just then, the door opened. "Housekeepi—oh!" said the room attendant, astonished by the sight of the blue-skinned man. Sand turned and Karl lunged for the gun. Emil and Chaissie burst in through the open door and helped Karl wrestle the gun from Sand's hands and overpower him.

"All right, all right, get off me. I'll stand down," conceded Sand, as the attendant picked up the phone with trembling hands and called for hotel security.

A minute later two hotel security guards arrived and escorted Sand out of the hotel and into custody. A few minutes later, six police officers arrived and moved everyone from their rooms into the hall.

A half-hour later, a bomb squad arrived and carried two large boxes out of the commander's room, along with a pair of transponders. Surya said nothing, but nodded when they called for Sonya. In Arabic, she said they were there only to pray for His guidance and forgiveness.

The authorities held them for a few hours while they checked their identification. When it all checked out, they were let go. Sand and his team of munitions experts were not so lucky. By the time that the members of the A and B teams had secured passage back to America and were ready to check out of the hotel, the story of the thwarted American terrorist plot was all over the news.

* * *

Did you know?
The sudden and permanent disconnection from the 25th century's ever-present neural augmentation network led to the AI-deprivation dysphoria that scientists noted in the visitors they studied.

* * *

Karl and Li Yan had only been back home for a couple of days when Miran dropped by, for what she called a long-overdue visit. And as the three of them marveled at how very long it had been, a message arrived from an unknown party that said "Come out to your front driveway."

There was George, sitting in the driver's seat of a 20-foot cargo truck. When he saw Karl and Li Yan, he smiled. But when Miran appeared at the door, his jaw dropped.

He opened the door of the truck and stepped down onto the ground. He embraced them warmly. "Hey, check this out," he said as he led them around to the back of the truck. He unlocked the rear doors and opened them just wide enough to shine a flashlight inside. And there, concealed in the back of the customized rig beneath his homebuilt Faraday Cage, was the old prototype Bubblecraft.

Karl couldn't believe his eyes. "You have a Bubblecraft?"

George smiled. "I borrowed it from a friend."

"Hey," George said to Karl. "Remember that idea you and

Li had for syncing to that old quantum radar signal from 1947?"

Karl's mind raced through through the crazy maze of all the failed experiments and algorithms he had tried over the years, hoping to reproduce the temporal teleportation effect he had somehow achieved that one disastrous day, when Miran's daughter Frigg was lost somewhere along the twisted path of space-time.

"I remember, but I'm afraid it's not a happy memory for any of us here."

"Well, I've been working on that, and I think I might be able to help."

"I really don't see how," Karl said glumly.

"Li Yan," said George, "you must remember that idea you sent me, where you were playing around with the concept that Susan Everett's original temporal equation used six dimensions, but which we ended up compactifying into five? Remember how you were wondering whether all six might really be required? It was that idea you had—that there might be something like two enantiomorphic universes with opposite arrows of time—that got me thinking: if we knew exactly when and where that quantum radar signal was occurring, we could lock onto it and run an enantiomorphic algorithm against it."

"We *do* know that," said Li Yan. "We got that information from the *Project Looking Glass* report."

"That is great news," George chortled. "I've got a firmware version running on this beast that just needs those time-space coordinates, and we should be able to lock onto that and get all tangly with it, so to speak."

"You mean there might be a chance, after all, to get temporal displacement working on an event in the past?"

"Well, we managed it once, didn't we?"

"Hmm, *Project Looking Glass*, you say? Just a moment," said George. "I'm running a search for... Ah, here it is. Oh, yeah—that was a whole series of leaked reports and records about those radar tests from the 1940s and '50s wasn't it? And... bingo! I did a search for 'blue skin' and found an interesting record here. Look at the name."

"Oh my god. Frigg! That's gotta be her. Does it say where she was found?"

"Yep. It says she was 'recovered' alive in July 1947 and was in a military lab called 4B for quite a while after that. Uh, unfortunately, it looks like Leonid didn't survive. It says a male companion was found dead at the scene. But get this— 'the scene' was not in Washington state. Not even close. It says here she was found about 26 miles southeast of Corona, New Mexico."

"No, that can't be right."

"I'm telling ya, man, that's what it says here."

"I do want to caution you," interjected Li Yan. "Almost every theorist out there who ever dared to consider the possibility that we might someday get reverse time travel working is seemingly convinced that it might seriously mess up our reality or fracture the timeline. You know, the butterfly effect and all that. So, changing the past is probably a really dangerous thing. And not to mention: I'm not sure we want to be seeing crowds of time travelling tourists at, you know, the crucifixion or whatever, right?"

"But those leaked documents mentioned that the so-called Roswell alien was named Frigg, right? There couldn't have been much—if any—impact to the timeline in the first place, if it was all top-secret stuff. None of that stuff was ever confirmed or made public, so it may or may not have happened at all. It's an extremely limited branch of the timeline."

"Ah yes, it says she was transferred to a location on the Roswell army base named 'medical building 4B' later that night. That's another 59 miles or so on down to the southeast."

"I should be able to look up the floor plans and building permits for that, just a minute..." said Li Yan.

"So, if we can get the exact coordinates of that area of the base, we might be able to jump straight there, inside the perimeter of the base, or maybe even right into the building."

"You say 'we' like you think I'd go on a crazy-sounding mission like that."

"I'll go with you," offered Miran.

"Whoa. Slow down. There are lot of moving parts we have get moving in the right direction before anybody is jumping anywhere."

"Hm, okay, I think I've got those coordinates for you. The exact coordinates of that area of medical building 4B *should* be: 33.3306743746205, -104.50760853385356—assuming this old floor plan is correct. At the very least, those parameters should get us inside the secure perimeter."

"You say perimeter and I say parameter..."

"Why can't we just jump back to a point a few minutes

before the accident happened and just move Frigg and Leonid off the platform, or, I don't know, stop Karl from pushing the button in the first place?"

"Believe me, I wish I could do that," said Karl. "It requires a very specific kind of signal that the US military was experimenting with back in 1947. We can sync to that signal, but we had nothing like that running in our lab, so we can only jump to where the signal was, while it was active."

"Except that doesn't explain why she ended up in New Mexico instead of Washington State."

"There might have been a bug in the compensation values for the earth's angle and speed of rotation," suggested Karl. "I'd better double-check that part of the code."

Later...

"Oops. I found the error. It was that buggy vector offset routine that Marjorie Blint figured out the solution to. Note to self: coding mission-critical routines while sleep-deprived leads to stupid mistakes. Okay, I think it should work correctly this time."

"To minimize the chance of losing George's 'borrowed' Bubblecraft, I've set it to auto-return here if the failsafe time limit is exceeded—I'm setting that to five minutes." Do you think that's enough time?"

"Honestly, I'll be surprised if we have even half that much time to find her and get her out of there alive. And you'd better be prepared that one or more hostiles might be onboard when it does return. They could show up right here, armed and dangerous. So be prepared for that."

He handed Miran a white lab coat. "Here, put this on."

"Why?"

"It might not do any good, but there are probably doctors in a place called 'Medical lab' and if dressing like one reduces the chance that we'll be shot on sight, well, that's worth a try, I think."

"We're not going to fool anyone. We all have blue skin," Miran reminded him.

* * *

Karl initiated the startup sequence from the control ring's command panel and watched the status lights until they were all green. "All right. Signal sync established. Power level is good. Are you ready to go?"

"Ready as I'll ever be."

"You realize that we'll be jumping onto a military facility where they have orders to shoot first and ask questions later, right?"

"I understand."

"And if they don't kill us, they'll capture us if they get half a chance."

"I get it. It's risky. It's my daughter. Let's go."

George backed the truck closer to the garage, then Karl and Miran climbed into the back of the truck and got into the Bubblecraft. Karl pulled the control ring down into position and powered up the onboard systems. Sitting at Karl's workbench in the garage, George ran through the initialization sequence and gave them the thumbs-up when it was complete.

"Okay. Keep your hands and arms inside the control ring when the craft is in operation. I've set the coordinates for what should be the middle of medical room 4B. Statistically, people spend less time in the exact center of a room than any other location in it, so it should be reasonably safe. And with any luck, we'll be in and out of there before any of the guards see us."

"But there must be surveillance cameras."

"Not necessarily. This was an ancient time, before there were video cameras. So, there's still some risk of discovery if she is under direct surveillance, but we probably don't have to worry about an automated alarm scenario. No one's going to expect her to escape without leaving the room. Remember, we'll have to jump straight back here if we're detected or attacked."

"You keep your finger on the jump button. I'll get her into the craft."

"It's going to be a tight fit. Be sure she's inside this control ring. If she's not completely within it, bad things will happen."

"Ready?"

Miran nodded. "Let's do this."

Blink.

The craft materialized in the middle of the room not far from the bed Frigg was sitting on.

Miran leapt from the craft and pulled the startled girl toward to her feet. "Come quickly," she whispered.

The door flew open and a guard lunged at Frigg. Karl pulled Miran, who was holding on to Frigg for dear life, closer to him and punched the jump button. The guard's hands were inside the control ring, but the rest of his body was outside.

"Auggh!" His body rapidly aged and turned to dust, leaving only a pair of withering hands.

Miran hugged Frigg. They were back in the truck.

Karl smiled as the controller completed its post-run diagnostic sequence and powered down. George looked triumphant. He looked over at Li Yan, her thumbs up.

"Are we ready to send the success signal to McChord?" she asked.

"Absolutely. We just have to make sure that there's no persistent record of what has just transpired."

"Got it."

Li Yan typed % rm -rf / and hit Enter.

"Done."

THE END
of Book 3

Afterward

3001

Now *this* is interesting, thought the machine. Is it possible that some exquisitely elegant, generalized truth permeates all creation, all invention, that what is true at the microcosmic level is true also for the macrocosm?

Across the holographic panels scrolled connections between disparate elements: from the projects of Da Vinci emerged his "corkscrew" helicopter design and the architecture of the double-helix-shaped Grand staircase of Chambord.

The designs of the corkscrew and the helix rotated and, when viewed from the top, became a yin-yang symbol. And then the components of the double helix began to deconstruct and reorder themselves: the sixty-four DNA codons of the genetic code mapped exactly one-to-one to the sixty-four hexagrams of the ancient Chinese system *I Ching*, as symbols of the *Unus Mundus*.

○ ○ ○

Did you know?

The extraordinary fact that the *I Ching* and the sixty-four DNA codons are exactly the same when written in binary order provided the topic of the funeral address given by Carl G. Jung in honor of the great German translator of *I Ching*, Richard Wilhelm.

○ ○ ○

HELIX

In Book One, mathematician Susan A. Everett, intrigued by Einstein's statement that time "is like space"—that is, not just a single dimension—guides a team of researchers to a breakthrough reinterpretation of his famous space-time theory. This, along with code developed by an AI-based programming genius, unlocks the secret of time travel, but in the forward direction only. What they don't know is how their experiments affect the future world. The story focuses on the life-changing experiences of the first people to go forward, when there's no going back.

HAVEN

In Book Two, corporatism catches up with a ruthless executive when an AI entity replaces him as CEO of a leading tech company. Meanwhile, his radicalized son and a brilliant programmer steal the world's most valuable intellectual property: a top-secret device capable of communicating with the future. These revelations result in a cult-like following for a mysterious prophet. Is it the beginning of a new world order? This is the story of what happens next, at the end of time.